Hunting Paradise

Bob Henneberger

www.temptpress.com

Books by Bob Henneberger

Crackstone Chronicles – Extinction

Crackstone Chronicles – Connections

Crackstone Chronicles – Extraordinary Solution

Katz Pajamas

Katz Box

Katz Cradle

Tempt Press
PO Box 77
Colchester, VT 05446

Published by **Tempt Press**
P.O. Box 77, Colchester, VT 05446

First Print Edition, 2010

Copyright © 2010 Bob Henneberger

ISBN: 978-0-9830118-0-4
Library of Congress Control Number: 2010936729

To Sandy

Tis not enough to help the feeble up, but to support them after.

Preface

In the middle of the journey of our life,
I found myself again in a dark wood,
that the straight way was utterly lost.
Alas how hard it is to say what it was like,
this savage and sharp and strong forest,
which even in thought renews my fear!
So bitter was it that death is little more so;
but in order to speak of the good that I found there,
I'll tell of the other things I saw there.

Dante Alighieri, **Inferno**, *Canto 1*

Chapter 1

We sometimes congratulate ourselves at the moment of waking from a troubled dream; it may be so the moment after death.
Nathaniel Hawthorne Passages from the American Notebooks (1868?), entry for 25 Oct. 1836

Wind moving through the forest masked most animals' sounds, except for five crows chattering in a pine tree next to the river. A solitary hawk circled on a warm thermal searching for her next meal. As the thermal pushed the hawk higher into the sky, she could see the river as it meandered through thick woods. She dove for a mouse on the riverbank, then flew away, wings laboring with her prize. The water flowed almost silent, except for an occasional gurgle, where the chocolate muddy current folded under a partially sunken branch. Fall still lingered in the trees and thickets, light to dark earth tones, randomly spattered with bright yellow orange and red. Further from the banks, the terrain heaved into rumpled mounds of browns and greens piled like unkempt blankets on the ground. The forest grew no more than a half mile to a mile from the bank in both directions. Beyond the forest lay vast areas of cleared and plowed farm land.

For a mile and a half along the river, the forest was owned and managed by several families who owned the mill. They had cleared only enough trees to build a dozen homes to house them all, plus a ten acre garden to raise food and support their two milk cows, five horses and thirty chickens. The locals called the mill and its clutch of houses the Rose Community, named for the family who bought the land in 1849 and built the mill. Abraham Rose and his brother Hezekiah had moved from

Pennsylvania to establish a religious community here, free from slavery.

On the border of the garden plot, two boys stooped over a well used plow as they struggled to right it and move it to a small barn one hundred yards away. They had been asked to clean the plow, oil it, then store it for the winter. Both of them had felt a great sense of relief when the other boys, along with two men, set out in the community wagon to collect dead and downed hardwood for fuel. In the coming weeks they would have to cut and split the wood, but for today they had the easier chore.

Paul smiled, looking into the woods as he talked. "I don't know if I want to stay on here forever. I like this place well enough, it don't want to eat you up like plantation land."

"Wonder what bein' that rich would feel like," Mark stood up and wiped his brow.

"My mama has a piece of paper in her old trunk that says I owned fifty acres." Paul used hushed tones, as if giving away a deep family secret. "I saw it yesterday when mama was out workin' in the mill. I remember living on that spot of land when I was small, but I didn't know it was mine. She doesn't know I can read that well, but I read it all. She also has a piece of paper signed by a doctor." He paused again. "I think it's about me."

"That's nothing special." Mark focused on the first thing his friend had said. "I want to know about that land you said you owned, that fifty acres."

"It was where I was before me 'n my folks came up here," Paul stared in the distance. "I remember it was near town, in the bottom land close to the road."

"That's a good piece of land," Mark replied. "Was it near the thick woods?"

"Right on the edge of it," Paul confirmed, still not looking at Mark. "I thought we share cropped on it, until Mr. Appleby threw us off it."

"And, you seen the piece of paper that says you owned it?" Mark skeptically asked. "You sure it's real?"

8

"Don't know," Paul answered with a shrug. "Might be, but it don't matter no way."

"Why not?"

"No one would let me or my mama own that good a piece of land no way," Paul replied.

"Maybe someone would." Mark tried to sound encouraging.

"Sarah Bellows was my real mama, if one of those pieces of paper in my mama's trunk tells the truth."

"Who's that?"

"She married that Appleby man who owns all the old plantation land," Paul said, slowly sounding out the name.

"The Appleby who owns all that land, the same man who threw you off yours?" Mark's replied, somewhat startled.

"The same one," Paul answered. "I guess we wasn't wanted there; all that land never will be mine, but if what I read is true, at least I know what should be."

"You white?" Mark sounded unsurprised. "We thought you was, partially so at least."

"Recon so, but ain't nobody gonna believe it," Paul replied.

"God, you were that close to owning all that land!" Mark held up his hand to show a small space between his thumb and forefinger.

"Not that close."

"Did your mom ever say anything about the Appleby woman before?"

"No, she didn't say much about her time on the plantation, and after my Dad died, she didn't say nothin'," Paul answered.

"I don't want to leave this place." Mark nodded his head for emphasis. "I grew up here, even my Yankee parents wouldn't leave, they love the land too much."

"I don't know," Paul tilted the plow back on its wheel so they could drag it to the barn. "I think I'd like to see what else is out there; there ain't too much here for me, near as I see it."

9

"There's me, and all your other friends and your mama."

"I guess," Paul mused.

"This dang plow is put away now." Mark closed the barn door behind them. "What say you and me go do somethin' else before the rest of them get back from collectin' wood."

"Sure."

"What about huntin' some deer?" Mark sounded excited. "I was walking up by the beaver swamp on Harris Creek a couple a days ago and I saw a whole lot of them there."

"Sure." Paul nodded quickly. "Will your father let you borrow the Enfield?"

"I don't see why not." Mark hesitated. "I brought home the last batch of deer meat and my mom was happy to have it."

"Can we make it back to home in time for dinner if we get a big ol' buck?"

"Don't see why not." Mark paused to think. 'It's about ten in the mornin' and the swamp isn't but a mile from here."

Paul nodded and let out a burst of air, then raced Mark toward the houses.

....

"This place don't feel like it usually does," Paul looked up and down the shore line of the small creek.

As the two boys left the village and mill, bright sunshine had shone overhead, but by the time they reached this thick woods by Harris Creek, a thin layer of clouds darkened the landscape. Paul was wearing his gray coat with the tear on the left sleeve. He had tried to sew it together, but it still flailed a small shred of cotton as his arms swung.

"What're you talkin' about?" Mark asked. "It looks the same as I left it two days ago."

"Yeah, I know," Paul answered his friend. "But, somehow it feels different, like someone's out there."

"Ain't nobody here." Mark pointed towards the beginnings of the swamp. "Could be the clouds movin' in."

Several small beaver dams interrupted the creek about a half mile down stream. The bottom land flooded all too often, so planting crops on it was uncertain at best but the dams kept more good farm land from flooding so the local farmers wisely left them alone. The beaver pond also attracted enough small game to keep the locals well fed throughout the year, so the swamp stayed, and that particular patch of forest was left alone. It was the only reminder of what the land had looked like for the millennia before the white man came. It would remain, without further change for some time to come.

"Sure feels like there's somebody here to me," Paul insisted. "No matter, where did you see those deer the other day?"

"They was walkin' from this side of the creek up to the top of that hill over there, then down towards the river." Mark pointed to a small knoll with a thick stand of river beech and a few chestnuts.

"Best we get to the high ground beyond the hill up there." Paul trudged towards the stand of beech trees. "The way the wind's blowin' we got to get down wind of any deer comin' this way."

"I'm right behind ya." Mark slung the musket over his left shoulder and followed Paul up the hill. As they walked, a fog began to envelop the woods.

"Look at all the deer track," Paul observed. "There's some big ones passed through here for sure."

"Like I said." Mark proudly added, pointing to a dense stand of mixed trees. "Let's set up somewhere up there and get us a big buck."

"What time you reckon it is?" Paul asked.

"By the sun, I suppose it's about one," Mark guessed. "We can stay out here an hour or two, then we got to get back home."

11

"Yeah, that's what I thought," Paul replied. "If it gets much more cloudy, or starts to rain, I want to get goin' sooner. It's getting' cold."

Mark nodded, then he paused, looking for the best cover in which to wait for a deer.

"How about over there." Mark pointed to a stand of pine saplings which stood three feet tall at best.

"Why don't you put a load in the musket now," Paul said.

Mark picked up his rifle and plucked a paper wrapped cartridge from a leather pouch hanging under his left arm. Pulling out the ramrod, he tore off the powder end of the cartridge then poured the gun powder down the barrel. With the end of the ramrod, Mark jammed the lead bullet still wrapped in the greasy paper down the barrel. After pulling the hammer back one notch, he carefully installed a percussion cap on the nipple.

"You gotta be pissed about all that land bein' taken from you 'n your folks," Mark said.

"I guess I am." Paul reluctantly sat down next to his friend. "I don't feel that mad, though."

"I would be," Mark paused. "I mean if a bunch of yahoos rode in and took all my daddy's land away."

"But, I didn't know it belonged to us until yesterday." Paul sighed. "If my folks had told me about it before, I might be all worked up."

"And, that paper that says your real mama was white?" Mark added. "What you think about that?"

"I don't think much of it," Paul paused. "It don't matter no way, ain't no white man gonna accept me as one of his."

"My daddy does."

"He's different."

"After you think on it some more, you might feel different," Mark assured him.

"Maybe." Paul fell silent.

"So, does this change your plans?" Mark didn't want to change the subject, but for his friend's sake he did. "I mean, you still thinkin' about travelin'?"

"Yeah," Paul answered. "More than before."

"Where?" Mark asked. "Still out west?"

"I think I'd like to go on to California eventually."

"That sure sounds like fun," Mark said, fascinated by the thought. "I'd love to go with you, but I want to stay here and work with my dad."

"You always say that." Paul chuckled. "Your brother is more likely to go with me."

"Could be, but I don't think any of the Rose kids will ever leave this place." Mark leaned back. "We all like it here too much."

"I can't see that," Paul politely objected. "This place is not that good to us."

"It could be worse," Mark said, looking away.

"It could be a whole lot better." Paul started to say more, then stopped. "Why don't we keep quiet; the deer will never come near us if we keep on flappin' our jaws."

The two boys shifted their positions slightly, then settled down to wait. At one point Mark stole a sideways glance at Paul, but decided to say no more.

…………………………

A sharp noise made them jump, although they were too well trained to move about. The rifle blast filled the woods; the shot immediately echoed off the hills, dampened a bit by the surrounding trees. Both boys looked in all directions, as if they were trying to spin their heads three hundred and sixty degrees at once.

"What the hell was that?" Mark demanded in a loud whisper.

13

"It was a rifle. But no rifle sounds like that, least wise none that I ever heard before, did you hear the loud cracking sound?"

"Sure was loud," Mark agreed.

"What the hell was it?" Paul asked, keeping his voice quiet.

"Maybe one of those fancy new huntin' rifles with the brass cartridges." Mark was still peering into the trees. "But, where?"

"Came from over there." Paul pointed to their north. "I told you other people were here."

"I guess you was right. What do we do now?"

"We could go on back," Paul replied. "I don't like the feel of this place."

"Let's see if they got a big buck," Mark said. "Sure as hell won't get one around here after all that noise."

"I don't know." Paul paused, then looked at the ground. "This makes me feel funny. I think we better go on back home."

"I wanna go see the deer they shot."

"You ain't goin' over there, are you?"

"Sure I am," Mark insisted. "I want to see one of those new huntin' rifles up close."

When Paul hung back, silently, Mark shouted, "Hey, mister. Did you get a buck?"

"Who is that." Ahead of them a voice called back. "Is that one of you?"

"It's me," Mark shouted. "Mark Rose from down by the mill."

"What mill?" The voice shouted back.

"'Bout a mile or so up the river from here," Mark answered.

They could still see no one.

"Don't tell them where we live," Paul whispered. "They could be Klan or something."

"We're lost out here," the voice shouted. "Can you help us find the town?"

14

Mark walked towards the voice. "Sure thing, where are you now?"

"I can't hear you, you must be walking away from me."

"I ain't gone nowhere." Mark looked at Paul. "Hello!" he called out as he faced a new direction.

"You trust strangers too much," Paul whispered angrily. "Let's get home and send some help out for them."

"Where'd you go?" the strange voice shouted, still loud but now a little hollow, like an echo.

"I'm getting scared." Paul tugged at Mark's sleeve, motioning him to stop.

"I bet his voice is bouncin' off the hills around here." Mark looked at his friend. "Maybe we can hear him, but he can't hear us."

"Could be." Paul didn't want the stranger to find them. At that moment, it started to rain, falling as a cold, heavy mist. "Let's get back home 'n tell them about these lost strangers."

Mark ignored him, he shouted again, "Hey mister, we'll send someone back later."

When several more attempts failed, Mark agreed to go home and summon help.

"You told them we'd send someone to look for them," Paul reassured him.

"Let's get goin'." Mark agreed.

The boys turned to the north and began walking as fast as they could. The rain steadily increased, making the cold feel more brutal as the boys became soaked. They discussed Mark's rifle, Paul handing Mark a heavy cotton shirt to wrap it in, then quickly pulling on his worn jacket.

"I figure you should fire off that bullet in the gun before the powder gets wet and you have to pull it out." Paul observed.

"Not a bad idea." Mark aimed the musket at the ground and fired it, he then wrapped the gun in Paul's shirt, covering as much of the rifle as he could.

15

The two boys paused to catch their breath; they had made it back to the river, and the path along the eastern bank that led straight to the mill.

"It's not too far to go," Mark said. "Who do you think that hunter was? "

"He couldn't have been from around here, or he wouldn't be lost," Paul replied, between gulps of cold air. "If he were he wouldn't be lost."

"I guess not," Mark agreed. "He didn't sound like no Yankee." He huffed a bit as they increased their pace. "He sounded like he was from town, like a good 'ol boy."

"That's the problem." Paul began to walk faster.

Mark gave him a startled glance.

. . . .

Ruth Rose shook her head, only slightly disapprovingly at her son and Paul as they stood inside the front door to the cabin. "You boys are wet as two frogs in a pond."

"I'm sorry, Ma," Mark replied, looking sheepishly at his mother. "It didn't look like rain when we left."

"No, it didn't," His mother agreed as she tossed two towels to them. They began to strip down, gratefully getting into drier clothing as fast as they could. The boys told her the story of the lost hunter whose voice had disappeared; she shook her head.

"It's real thick around there," Ruth said. "No one ever did clear that whole area; it's always been too swampy and it floods all the time."

"Yeah, but there's only about a hundred acres that's not cleared for cotton around there." Mark ran the towel around his wet hair. "It'd take a lot of dumb to get lost in that small a forest."

"I guess some of the men folk could head out that way after church services tomorrow," Ruth said. "It won't take that long to find them if they're still in there."

16

"That'd be the kind thing to do," Paul agreed. "Someone has to look after those who can't look after themselves."

"Could you please dump those wet clothes on the front porch," Ruth sighed. "I want you two to hang them on the line out back if it's sunny tomorrow. I suppose we can do some wash later this week, but they'll be fine if you dry them out."

"Oh, it's almost stopped rainin'." Mark pulled on a pair of dry shoes. "I got to clean Pa's rifle real quick before it sets up rusting."

"I guess you'd better." Ruth turned around and stared at her son and Paul. "You go on and clean the rifle, Paul can help me get dinner ready."

"Where's Pa?" Mark grabbed the rifle and headed back to the covered front porch.

"He's with your brother and some other men down at the mill," Ruth answered. "A big load of grain was brought in today and the gentleman is in somewhat of a hurry to leave."

....

A road from the southern end of the Rose Community led to a river crossing, sometimes manned, sometimes not. A large raft made from logs was tied to a rope loop which spanned the river. On both sides of the river, the rope loop was fixed to sturdy trees by a pulley. This crossing was the closest entrance and exit to the community from the nearby town. Visitors were first greeted by the well tended garden plot and clutch of houses, then by the mill and broad river.

The Rose Community was built near the river's extensive east bank. Since the land was cleared for the grist mill decades ago, cavernous runoff ravines burrowed deep into the sloping hills. Upriver lay a village which had a college, and downriver lay a larger town which served other small farms, as well as the nearby Bellows' plantation. Near the mill, musty smells from decades of rotting vegetation intermixed with the forest smell.

17

Dark came slowly to the Rose Community that night; a gentle rain subsided before sunset. Changing to the northwest, the wind picked up as a waning moon darted in and out of fast moving clouds. Cleared by a rapidly moving pacific cold front, the cold air magnified the starlight. Strong gusts pushed the trees from the west, the tallest of them undulating, gradually twisting as they first flowed with the wind, then gently sprung back; their tops set up a slight elliptical motion as the process continued.

Mark had to explain why he didn't come home with a quartered deer and his father took delight in teasing him. Dinner passed quietly.

Around nine in the evening, shouting men on horseback attacked the community without warning. They set it afire. Roaring flames merged with the pounding horse hooves and yelling figures, noises driven with a rage of fear. Few men from the Rose Community fought back directly; some helped the women and children escape the flames while others formed a ragged bucket brigade bringing water to the fires.

From inside their cabin, Paul watched the onslaught. The many imperfections in the window glass made the scene look dream-like, unfocused in the dim light. People moved like apparitions. Accenting the disorder, orange flames with jagged red fingers shot head high through doors and windows of several shattered buildings,.

Paul's mother, Mary, ran the length of the dirt street howling at the Klansmen, "You bastards! You bastards!"

Her arms flailed in the air. Drained more by despair than anger, Mary propelled herself after one, then another rider. When she paused to catch her breath, one Klansmen raised his heavy wooden torch, crashing it on her head. The flames on the end of the torch shattered into hundreds of small sparks that showered Mary with fire. The rider pulled in the reins of his horse and darted off in the direction of the mob as Mary fell, her dress smoldering.

Staring out the window, Paul felt everything slow down. Most of the able bodied had gathered to fight the fires, at the far end of the village. No one was near enough to put out the embers on Mary's dress. Paul found himself outside, staring at his mother. His awareness stepped out of time; the daylight of reality and this dark dreamlike scene blended. Taking off his coat, he wrapped her in it, smothering all the embers; through it all she moaned, muttering no comprehensible words. He left Mary wrapped up, lying in the street. Still dazed, he wheeled in slow motion towards the house.

Once indoors he sat down again in front of the distorted window glass. Time slipped away from him again. Fallen into a shallow trance, he stopped noticing details, his consciousness no longer registered the violence outside. Staring blankly ahead, he spoke in a whisper, "Only thing we have in common is blood soaked land, but what part is my part? Them shooting and busting up the place, us outlasting them, for a hundred years, it's still a war, it will always be a war. And no one ever understands why, even when they say they do."

He looked onto the floor, then fixed his lower jaw. "This ain't my war. This ain't my land, not now, not ever!"

A woman screamed. At the noise, Paul rose, like a wounded old man, to look through the door. Ahead of him, Ruth Rose was running toward the house, behind her was Zeke, her youngest son.

"Paul." Her voice quivered. "We saw you out there, your mother, the others are with her now. Mary will be all right, she's not badly burned." She broke into tears.

Meanwhile, a sullen silence spread through the streets, overlaid by continued explosions, fire and collapsing, burning buildings. As quickly as they had stormed the village, the mounted men left it. They gathered at the far end of the dirt road, near the road toward town. Milling about on horseback, they began to race towards the river crossing, heading back out of town.

Still weeping, Ruth had begun to sob in gasps. The thought came to her that she didn't want the young boys to suffer more by witnessing her grief, so she fled into her bedroom, shutting the door. In shock, she wasn't thinking clearly; it would take weeks for her reason to return completely. Zeke, Mark's younger brother, sat huddled beside Paul, on the floor. Suddenly, a chill rose along Paul's spine. He knew that some other bad thing had happened.

His mind rushed back to the Klan lynching of his father, John. The time of night three years ago, the smell of smoke, was all the same. Images of that night attack twitched in and out of his thoughts; the silent men on milling horses staring at his father's lifeless body. Faceless in the act, the killers felt alive only through another's death. That night had also ended with a hushed conference among the masked murderers. Although they had only been in this village once before, both times they reveled silently in their rites of blood.

"What happened?" Paul asked softly, not really wanting to know.

Mark's brother replied as if he were in a stupor, his voice took on the air of a disillusioned cantor, mindlessly repeating words with a metered, emotionless voice.

"Mark tried to run fast, he really did, but he stopped to push Mother into a ditch. You know, the ones the men dug at the end of the street to keep the rain water from washing away the road bed so bad. He run as fast as he could, but this big man on a spotted horse run him down."

Zeke took a big gulp of air. "He pushed Mark with the horse 'till he fell down, then Mark lay there, looking up at the man on his big horse. The man was carryin' the biggest sword I've ever seen, it was real wide at the hilt, and it was long as I've ever seen. He waited 'till Mark tried to stand up, then, without sayin' anythin', he swung that shiny sword down at Mark so hard it was almost like he threw it at him." Zeke fell silent.

"Mark?" Paul squinted his eyes, squeezing small tears from the corners.

"His head come clean off, it fell over from his neck, lots of blood comin' out of his neck pushed it over, it spun clean over and landed upright in the dirt right next to his body. It looked like he was buried in the ground, right there like you plant a new tree, his face looked real funny, it looked like he was tryin' to yell or scream, or somethin' like that, 'cept there weren't no sound, it was real funny lookin'. Dad and some of the older boys are takin' care of Mark now," Zeke abruptly fell silent again.

I'm in a nightmare and I can't wake up, Paul thought. He lowered his head into the palms of his hands and wailed. Ruth emerged from her room as their crying grew louder. She gathered both boys, one under each arm; the three of them sat together, they clutched each other in tearless silence for a long time.

…………………..

Several elders from the Rose Community met with the sheriff. They gave detailed accounts of the murder of Mark Rose; some Klansmen were recognized and identified by eyewitnesses. Polite to the point of contrition, the sheriff took all the information on the murder from the citizens of the Rose Community but started no actual investigation, made no arrest. Whether from fear or shame, the night riders never again visited the Rose Community after the death of Mark Rose.

…………………..

"It's only been a week since the riders came here," Ruth pleaded with Mary Burns. "Your son needs his mother."

"I can't do it no more," Mary's voice disappeared into the background.

"You have to be here for Paul," Ruth insisted. "He loves you so much."

"I don't think so," Mary mumbled. "Not since he found out about who he really is."

"You know that doesn't mean a thing to him." Ruth calmly put her hand on Mary's shoulder. "You and John raised him, you two are his parents."

21

"I can't do it no more," Mary repeated a little louder than before. "I do love that boy, but I can't live here no more."

"You and Paul are safe here," Ruth assured. "Where would you go?"

"I want you to look after Paul. You and Abraham are good people, and you and Paul are all white folk." Mary bitterly looked up at Ruth. "I lost my husband here, and you lost your son to them mean crackers." She paused. "I can't stay here no more."

"Where can you go, then?" Ruth asked.

"I'm goin' back to the plantation land," Mary said. "At least there I can be safe; ain't no one gonna kill me for workin' the land like my people's done for generations."

"They could and probably would kill you," Ruth disagreed. "You know Mr. Appleby has it out for you."

"As long as I play the good little slave girl, he ain't gonna do nothin'," Mary said. "It means I gave up and he won."

"What about your son?" Ruth asked again. "You should stay here."

"Paul needs to get as far away from this place as he can and as fast as he can," Mary's voice grew stronger. "Appleby's more inclined to kill him, not me. It's too late for me to get away from all this trouble, but it's not too late for him."

"He's welcome to stay here with us." Ruth didn't know what to say.

"I want to be buried near my mama, and that means I have to go back there and take up my old life in the field."

Leaving Paul with Ruth and Abraham Rose, Mary felt herself drawn back to the Appleby plantation like a ghost to darkness, going through the half forgotten tasks, as if dancing to familiar tunes. Six months after leaving the Rose community, she died, never speaking of her adopted son, Paul, again.

Chapter 2

O, call back yesterday, bid time return.
William Shakespeare Richard II, act 3, sc.2

Present day

They met, one by one, at Al Mozen's house for the start of their annual hunting trip; each of the men began with their own expectations. So far, this was exactly as their trips began for the past ten years.

The four men fell silent as the tires crunched over the gravel in Al's driveway. The house was about one hundred yards from the road and up a slight incline on the eastern edge of his thirty five acre farm. On the adjoining sixty acres, Al's brother, sister-in-law and three nephews ran a small dairy operation.

A large man, Al Mozen stood about six feet tall and two hundred seventy pounds, with a growing midsection. He wore short cropped hair, slightly longer than a crew cut, and a salt and pepper close cut beard. Sixty one years old, he had, outside of a two year stint in the Army, never lived anywhere else.

The rise from the road to Al's house was not sharp, but water from any sizable rainstorm cascaded down it, washing out his driveway. The last load of gravel delivered was the largest size he could use without making it impossible to drive on; he hoped the larger gravel would turn his driveway into a slow waterfall, instead of a washed-out creek bed.

One of the tires slid on a large chunk of rock as the van slowed next to the shoulder of state road Eighteen.

"Before I pull out." Tim studied the faces of each of the other three in the van as he spoke. "Has anyone forgotten anything?"

Nobody spoke.

"Do we all have our hunting license?" Tim paused again, slightly raising his eyebrows. "Enough ammunition, toilet paper?"

John laughed from the back seat. "Al could always use leaves like he did last year."

"Beats using Time magazine like you did five years ago," Al said, chuckling at the recollection.

"Ha," Tim laughed. "I always thought that was a shitty magazine, anyway."

"Very funny, but I think we remembered it this year," Billy's voice carried a nasal, high pitched tone to it.

Both Tim and Billy were in their mid thirties, and both had a thin build. Tim was five feet eleven inches tall, while Billy was five seven. Both of them were clean shaven, but Billy always looked as if he had just woke from a two hour sleep after a long night of partying.

"Let's get going, I don't like the looks of the sky," John said, staring vacantly out the side window.

John was in his mid fifties and acted more like an absent minded professor than an assistant floor supervisor in the local plant. His appearance was as close as one can come to country camouflage; average height, average build, average coloring, average everything.

Tim maneuvered the van slowly into the road, turned to the right and accelerated. It was a short distance to the flashing yellow light and the turn onto state road fifty one; the shortest way to the forest was to skirt the city, then head Southeast.

On the road, the van cruised in lock step behind an eighteen wheeler. This state road was well traveled, even in the middle of a Friday afternoon. The houses lining the road had been other people's idea of the serene country life at one time, their decline unnoticed until inevitable transformations overtook them. Looking almost as a silent friend, to their right stood the empty manor house. Construction on this house had begun in eighteen twenty eight, with two additions built onto the massive structure over the next one hundred years. Then the boll weevil

24

drove the owners and any buyers away. At its present configuration, the plantation house still looked dignified, albeit empty and in great disrepair. Molting, two story white columns rose around three sides, topped by a massive roof that projected over the front, tiled porch. Most of the white paint had all but flaked off the house and columns, leaving bare wood on the north and west faces of the building. The roof still held most of its squared, flat black stones, although sizable cracks in the slate were visible even from the road.

When planters first built on the land, the old coach route originally ran more than a mile from this spot. The first paved version of state road fifty-one ran that original route; some of the bridge work which crossed Miller's creek remained, marking the old road bed. Thirty years before, the State had moved the road closer to the manor house, to avoid four long slow curves. Sitting on a small rise, the once great mansion now stood as a tired old giant looking at time passing it by.

"God," Tim remarked, breaking a long silence. "I'd love to have the run of that old thing for a few days, think of all the stuff that's been left in it over the years."

"Their ain't nothing' left there," Al remarked, shaking his gray head. "A real estate company bought it 'bout three years ago, but never moved in."

"Why not?" John asked.

"They figured it was too damned expensive to get it livable; I read 'bout it in the Sunday paper a few years ago. They wanted to completely refinish the inside and outside, but it was gonna be over a million bucks to do it all up right. They told 'bout all the stuff they found hidden away in there but they sold all the junk they found inside to some antique place in the city," Al paused while he strained a look out the rear window.

Behind them, the old house had disappeared, no longer visible through the sparse tree line next to the road.

"I wish I could've talked them into lettin' me tear it down for the lumber," Al added.

"What would you do with all that lumber, Al?" Billy asked.

Billy picked up a medium sized white Styrofoam cup and drooled a small wad of brown tobacco juice from the side of his mouth into the cup. A pungent smell of half digested tobacco leaves filled the van.

"It ain't for me, I'd sell it," Al answered, looking at Billy, who put the cup on the floor next to his feet and turned around. "People in the city pay a fortune for old flooring, the fancy trim work, and mantles, you could make enough off it to live on for years."

"That house deserves better than that." John quietly folded his arms across his chest. "And, I wish you'd not chew that crap in the car."

Billy turned to face John and silently grinned, showing teeth covered with brown aromatic juice.

"What?" Tim asked with a smile, not taking his eyes off the road in front of him.

"That house's been here since before the Civil War, it's seen a hell of a lot of history, and it deserves more than to be ripped apart for lumber, or a new shopping center," John said, a little louder. "It's been through more than any other building around here, and, like us, it's still here."

"I guess you're right," Al said softly. "I'd hate to see it go, it's a landmark; you know it's only twenty more minutes to the center of town when you pass it by, least ways if the traffic ain't too bad." Al paused for a breath. "It's been on that piece of land for such a long time, think of all the valuable stuff that's lost in the dirt under and around it, I'd like to at least give it a go with my metal detector for an afternoon."

"Now, that sounds like fun," Tim said. "I'd like to do that with you some day if we could get permission before they tear it down or something."

"Damned politicians in that city want to get rid of the damned thing that reminds 'em of the way it used to be," Billy coughed.

"You mean the black politicians?" John asked in a low baiting voice.

"Yeah, that's exactly what I mean," Billy said a little louder. "Anything 'bout the way it used to be, they want to tear down. Ya know, there's a lotta history they've gotten rid of 'round here." Billy rose slightly in his seat, then spat another wad into the white cup.

"I don't think the way the manor house has been treated means anything," John added, unfolding his arms. "Landmarks like that old house disappear because they're in the way of something else."

"Yeah," Tim half chuckled. "Like a used car lot."

"Run by the mayor's brother-in-law." Al laughed out loud.

"I think it'd be damned interesting to see an old plantation run like it was back in the day," Billy insisted. "Might even make some money."

Billy hunched back down into his seat.

"To change the subject, or at least to deflect it slightly." John paused. "My father used to work in the fields at that place during the summers, while he was in school." John looked at Billy who did not return the glance. "Maybe it wasn't like it used to be in the good old days, he wasn't a slave, he got paid for the field work, although he used to say he worked for a slave wage."

"I didn't know that." Tim glanced back at John for a moment. "I thought you said he was a doctor, or something like that."

"He was, but he picked cotton while he was in medical school," John replied. "He used to tell all of us about it. Some prominent family from around here brought it back to almost its original size."

"How many acres did they have?" Al asked quickly, with anticipation in his voice.

"My father said they had forty five thousand, it took all of this corner of the county, and spilled into the bordering two."

"What did they grow, mostly?" Billy asked, turning around to face John.

"Cotton, he said they also raised cattle, and kept a lot of pasture land for the cows and a few horses." John relaxed and leaned back into his seat. "My father also said that most of the land close to the house was in hardwood, they kept the farm operation away from the main house; the actual farming operations started from where the old slave town was."

"Forty five thousand acres." Billy slowly savored each word. "I can't imagine that much land belonging to one man."

"It doesn't," John interrupted.

"It did," Billy insisted, nodding his head once for emphasis.

"That's my point, it did, but it doesn't," John answered Billy. "They lost title to it all in the late thirties, after selling off half to support the remainder."

"How do you know so much about it?" Tim asked.

"My father told me," John paused. "He knew the family, he worked for them in the Summers for three years and he told us about it so often that my mom and I felt it happened to us as well as him."

"I've known you for ten years," Al puzzled. "And you've never told me any of this before."

"Yeah," Tim added. "Did your folks come from around here?"

"A long time ago, on my father's side," John answered. "He belonged to the land, like your people did."

"My people didn't belong to nothin'," Billy's tone turned indignant. "They was sharecroppers south of Madison, back there."

"Yeah," Tim spoke softly. "We know that, but I'm interested in John; when did your folks leave here and where did they live?"

"Around the plantation back there, then they moved south of here, around where we hunt. For years and years, that

28

place was the main economy for three counties," John answered. "But, my family moved up North a long time ago."

"You don't have no brothers or sisters, do you?" Tim asked. "I never heard you mention any."

"No." John hesitated slightly. "For one reason or another, my father's side of the family never had more than one child, going back at least three generations."

"Is that why you moved back here?" Al looked at John with his head slightly cocked to his right. "I mean some of your folks are from around here."

"I don't know." John looked out the window. "I guess that's the reason."

"Why didn't you stay up North with all your Yankee friends?" Billy teased.

John looked at the back of Billy's head, then answered, "I guess it's my home after all," John paused. "When life plays its tunes, you dance to the familiar ones."

"What the hell does that mean?" Billy turned around and glared at John.

"It means, there's no place like home."

"Okay," Billy huffed, then turned around looking through the front windshield again. "You never do say what you mean, no-how."

"What kind of work did they do?" Al asked.

"Who?" Tim asked.

"I was askin' John what kind of work his kin did back on the plantation."

"They worked the land," John answered. "Most everyone worked the land in those days, the fields were the one thing that everyone had in common, and the only thing at which most could make a living."

"Was they share croppers?" Al asked, his forehead furrowed as the question spread over his face.

"No," John replied. "They owned a little plot of land, south of the plantation, but still in its shadow."

"Went bust?" Billy asked in a short burst.

29

"Plainly put, and almost correct," John answered.

"I wish I could've inherited some land, anything over five acres," Billy mused. "Too bad your relatives lost it before you had a chance."

"I'm sure glad my folks kept our farm, me and my brother's got a nice place to live, and we ain't gonna let it get out of the family," Al said.

"Yeah," Tim interrupted. "Did you guys hear 'bout Walt?"

"No." Billy looked across the van at Tim. "What 'bout him?"

"Ol' Walt almost had a chance at a big place." Tim took in a deep breath. "His father-in-law died six months ago and he left his two hundred acres to Walt's wife, and her brother."

"So," Al said with half a breath. "What happened, did they split it, or what?"

"Walt and his wife wanted to split it, but the brother only wanted the money." Tim shook his head.

"So, why didn't they buy the brother out?" Billy asked.

"The brother wanted twenty five hundred an acre for it," Tim said. "Do you know where it is?"

"Yeah," Al answered quickly. "His wife's father lived 'bout twenty miles on up eighteen from me, off to the right a few miles."

"Off on a dirt road," Tim emphasized. "Only half of it's cleared, and there's a ten acre swamp on it."

"I know the place," Al added. "It ain't worth no more than eight, nine hundred an acre at best."

"What happened?" Billy asked.

"They tried to deal with the brother, but he wanted cash. Walt couldn't find no bank to lend that much money on it, so they had to lose it," Tim said in disgust.

"How's that?" Billy asked.

"The judge said they couldn't force a split of the land, they would have to sell it and then split the cash," Tim answered.

"Has it sold?" Al asked.

"Not yet," Tim answered. "But he can't use it, and he's gonna lose it."

"He could buy some land with his share of the cash when it sells," John said.

"I guess so, but it ain't gonna be the same," Tim said. "He can't buy as much land, and it's his wife's home place they're gonna lose."

"I guess so." John looked back out the window. "It's too bad his wife and her brother couldn't work it out."

"I hear they hate each other," Tim added.

"Why?" John asked.

"Don't know," Tim said with a shrug. "I never did know her people that much."

"I bet that story would make quite a yarn," John's voice trailed off.

None of the others were interested in that gossip anymore.

They were making good time. The road widened into four lanes, then a median strip wedged between the opposite pairs of lanes. The eighteen wheeler pulled further ahead of their van as expansion joints in the cement road surface set up a rhythmic thump which traveled from the tires to the interior seats, accompanied by a soft wave like movement a fraction of a second later. The four men rocked in silence for another five miles.

"Do you all still want to go to the creek, or do you want to try that back ridge?" John asked, looking out the front windshield. "I kind of like that ridge, the country's beautiful along that section," John paused for a moment. "You guys know that old dirt road with the historical marker on it?"

"Yeah, but I like the creek better," Al said.

"Me too," Tim added. "There's water, and it's way the hell out in the boonies where no one else wants to be."

Billy nodded in agreement before he entered the conversation, "I like being that far away from everyone else; it's safer, and I think there's more game there too."

"Okay, it looks like I'm out voted," John conceded. "We'll set up where we always do, but I hope we get set up before dark."

"That'll be a first," Al chuckled.

The van bounced the four silent men for another two miles.

"Janice's family owned all that land back there," John spoke up. "They owned a plantation about a mile back up the road from right here."

"Are you and your wife related or somethin'?" Billy abruptly asked. "You ain't supposed to marry your blood relations, Ya know."

A wicked grin crept onto Billy's face, it was a mean teasing grin.

"We aren't related by anything but marriage, and that's not why I brought it up." John looked blankly at Billy. "Her family started that plantation in the late eighteen thirties and she told me something interesting a few months ago about where we hunt."

"Well," Tim asked. "Don't stop now, what did she tell you?"

"The family that started her plantation, also owned all the land around where we hunt," John continued. "Do you remember that funny building down from the ridge, and the old foundation about a hundred yards from it?"

"Yeah," Al chimed in.

"There used to be a clear spring near by that everyone thought had the power to cure almost anything. Janice's ancestors bought it, built a Summer house there then they built that funny building around what used to be the springs. She said they had a big tile tub around where the water flowed out of the ground."

"Hey, that makes sense now," Al said. "I always wondered what that was all about."

"All the rich white planters from all around used to come and spend several weeks there to take the cure, and socialize. The women would gossip and the men would hunt, like we do now," John added.

"Only we ain't got no gossiping women with us," Al said.

"You're more talkative now," Tim said. "You ain't never told us about your ancestors that lived here."

"Yeah," Al added. "We always thought you came from Boston, or somewhere up there."

"My family lived in Wooster, which is sort of in the middle of the state," John paused. "But, my grandfather on my father's side was born and raised right here."

"I don't know the Barrington family." Al shook his head. "Did your kin have another last name then?"

"No."

"I sure don't remember any old families named Barrington around here." Al said.

"Me neither," Tim added.

"You got any more surprises 'bout yourself?" Billy half laughed.

"Not now." John quietly looked out the side window into the distance.

Next to the roadway, vast treeless tracts were home to shopping centers, condominiums, and professional buildings. Each mile closer to the city, the buildings grew in height. Pushed in from the horizontal, buildings grew in the vertical.

"This part of the trip's so ugly." Tim stared out the front windshield.

"I'd hate to have to live here," Billy said.

"We all could make a bundle more here than we do in the factory," Al said.

"It all evens out." John casually shrugged his shoulders. "You make more, you pay more to live; you get some convenience, you give up some."

"You're always the wise ass philosopher," Tim said in an annoyed voice.

33

"Sorry, when I hear anyone talking about choices, well, I'm reminded about mine. Remember, I used to live here in the city, after I first moved back down here," John said.

"You used to be a high school teacher, didn't you?" Al asked.

"I taught tenth grade English, and Biology when they needed it; both Janice and I were teachers in Massachusetts. I quit teaching here because I had to make more money when Janice got pregnant and she decided to quit working full-time to raise our daughter."

"But don't teachers make more money now?" Billy asked. "I mean more than a factory worker?"

"Not quite." John let out short breath. "I make more at the factory with you guys than some of my friends who stayed in the school system."

"Yeah, but you're an assistant supervisor," Billy huffed. "You make more than us common workers."

"I went to college for six years," John said, and chuckled. "That ought to be worth something."

"Not the way I see it," Billy responded.

"I still work the same hours you guys do, I have to rotate shifts like you do, and I get the same lack of respect from management you do," John insisted.

"Well," Al quietly interrupted. "Like you said, you made your choice then, but you still have choices now."

"And, I choose to go hunting with my friends," John paused. "At the creek site."

"All right," Billy said in a loud voice, taking a short punch at the air in front of him.

Tim slowed the van to forty five miles per hour then turned onto the third clover leaf exit. A shock of road signs greeted him as he slowed and stopped at a large stop sign; without looking at any of the signs, Tim turned left, driving less than one mile, he then turned left again onto state road seventy eight; this was the road which would take them into the forest.

34

They had come as far into the city as they needed; from this final turn, they passed from dense to scattered human population. As the old mansion was a sign post of one passage, this turn was the signal to the next.

"Forty five more minutes, tops, and we're there," Billy said triumphantly. "Tent pitched 'n everything."

"I hope so, look at the sky," John remarked, looking out the side window.

The whole sky had turned a slate gray, with charcoal streaks in it. The wind had picked up from the west, and now blew in heavier gusts.

"Turn on the radio," Al said. "Let's get some up to date weather."

"It don't work," Tim said with a loud sigh. "Don't some of you have transistor radios?"

"I didn't bring mine this year," Billy said. "John bitched so bad about my music last trip, that I didn't bring it."

"You have to admit, country music blaring out at nine o'clock at night isn't getting the feel of nature." John looked crossly at Billy.

"I ain't there to feel up nature, I'm there to get me some deer meat and a big damned Rack." Billy persisted, then picked up his Styrofoam cup to dribble some more tobacco juice.

"Don't you two get started again," Al broke in. "If we ain't got no radios, that'll be fine with me."

"If it gets much colder, we may all wind up sleepin' in the van tonight." Tim changed the subject.

"You could be right." John quietly sank back into his seat.

The houses facing the road began to have more space around them, that space was filled with trees, pastures and long lawns reaching to the shoulder of the highway. Other cars on the highway became fewer, and soon there was only an occasional vehicle.

The familiar places, those visited a few times a year, came in focus through the front windshield, then fell from view

35

through the rear window. The county line marker passed by the stares of the four men in the van. Eventually they reached two small creeks flowing under the same long bridge and the twin silos of a dairy farm. Framing everything was the forest, tree trunks randomly lined up like tall grass on a field for giants; pine, oak, poplars and beach, leaves just turning, green through orange, brown and red. Fallen leaves and needles lay as a carpet between the trees, young and old together.

"The woods are beautiful this time of year." Al looked through the side window next to his seat.

"I agree with that," Billy spoke softly. "This time of year in these woods mean a lot to me, especially this week."

"Me too," Tim agreed. "It sounds stupid, but it feels like us men have to get back to huntin' and bein' out here alone to get our heads back on straight."

"That's strange," Al joined in. "But I feel the same way too, it's somethin' like you said, Tim."

"What do you think, John?" Billy said, reluctantly. "Don't be too weird about it, though," he added in an undertone.

John paused, then spoke slowly. "When I sit alone in the cold woods, I see the land." He paused, looking into Al's puzzled face. "I see the space I'm in as never having changed; some farmer owns it, then sells it, they cut all the trees off it and raise crops, then the trees grow back, then the government takes it for a National Forest, then you and I sit on it and think it's ours."

"Stop blowing hot air out your ass and get to the point," Billy demanded, still looking out the front windshield.

"When I walk into the forest before dawn, I'm lost in the cold, dark woods, pursued by the wild animals of my dreams; I look for any familiar sign, then, usually one of you finds me stumbling around and shows me where my deer stand is."

Al chuckled, "Yeah, you have the worst time of all of us, finding your way in the dark."

"I settle down," John continued. "Lean back and fall into thought."

36

Billy snorted, and interrupted, "Get to the point." No one responded, and after a moment, John continued.

"Before any animal walked on the land, forests with tall vegetation were everywhere. No one owned it, no human saw it, and no human hunted in it," John paused. "Sometimes I imagine I'm in a different time, the forest has been through all ages and the forest knows us better than we know it. All I have to do is think of one particular time; I'd love to see and talk to the Indians who hunted these places five hundred years ago, of all the human spirits on this land, theirs is the strongest. As white men, we don't have them in our past to give us dreams, and that's our loss, it's a large hole in which many of us are lost. I also would love to see the first white men who farmed this land."

"You're gettin' weird." Billy muttered.

"Sorry, it's some of the English teacher left in me," John explained.

"That's okay," Tim said. "Sometimes I enjoy your weird stories."

"And some of us don't," Billy added, giving John a sideways sneer over his shoulder.

"Aw, leave him alone," Al said to Billy. "I think his ideas ain't so bad sometimes. I think I might do some of that day dreamin' this time." He paused. "It might make the time go faster, especially if I don't see no deer."

A short time later, they reached an intersection that bisected planted pine forest owned by a large paper company. Pine trees lined up in diagonal rows, as far as the eye could see from the road The highway department had placed a flashing red light at this spot, where the state highway and the U.S. highway crossed, three years before, after an accident which killed six people.

As Tim pulled the van away from the stop light, Al broke the silence, "How did you like teaching high school?"

"I liked it, and I miss it. I don't miss it that much, but I do miss it some," John replied.

"How hard is it?" Al asked

"God, that reminds me, did y'all hear what happened to Skeeter?" Billy interrupted.

John got a sour look on his face and said, "Yes, I heard."

"I can't believe he did it, do you?" Al smiled broadly.

"I wouldn't, but I kept a look out while they all did it," Billy said proudly.

"Will you three let me in on this," Tim demanded. "I don't know what happened."

"It was on last night's shift, you weren't there, you took the whole day off," Billy said.

"I remember that, what happened last night?" Tim demanded again.

"You know how Skeeter's been bragging on how big his dick is and how he's trying to get Peggy to go out with him," Billy tattled.

"Yeah, well, she called his bluff last night," Al said in a delighted voice.

"She what?" Tim asked.

John looked at Billy. "Peggy dared him to prove how long it was, in front of all the women on the shift, so on break, he did."

"He what," Tim shouted.

"Shit, it was better than that," Billy sounded annoyed at John. "Peggy, Beth, Carolyn, Ann, and Kelly took him into the women's room, along with a tape measure."

"You're kidding; Ann's got to be at least fifty years old. He stuck his thing out for her to see?" Tim asked in amazement.

"Beth said that Ann held his dick while Peggy measured it," Al chuckled like a thirteen year old.

"Yeah, and I kept watch while they was all in there." Billy said excitedly as he relived the incident. "I could hear'm laughin', and I could hear Skeeter swearing it could get bigger."

"Oh hell, why did I have to take the night off," Tim said. "Oh look, there's the National Forest boundary sign, we're almost to the turn off."

38

"Yeah." Al continued the story. "Carolyn said all they could get out him was five and a half inches, and Beth, Carolyn, and Ann all said their husbands' was longer than that."

"What did Skeeter say about that?" Tim asked.

"He claimed they couldn't get him hard, so it weren't no real measurement." Billy laughed.

"But," John interjected. "Skeeter will leave Peggy alone now, and that's what she wanted to happen in the first place."

"I guess so," Al laughed.

"Shit no," Billy insisted. "He asked her for another tape job right before the shift was up."

"Yeah?" Tim asked. "What did she say to that?"

"She said she'd keep lookin' for somethin' worth measurin'," Al answered.

"Yeah." Billy faced forward and leaned back in his seat.

"God." Tim shook his head, "That's a great story."

"I laughed my ass off," Al chuckled.

"And did you know what else I found out from Kelly?" Billy asked.

"I don't care." John looked out the side window at the scattered farm buildings.

"What?" Al asked.

"You were surprised at what Ann did, well, wait 'till you hear this," Billy teased.

"Don't drag this out, get to the point," Tim insisted.

"Well, she's been screwin' around on her old man," Billy loudly whispered.

"I'm not surprised," Al said.

"She's screwin' the shift supervisor on her break," Billy said in a louder voice.

"That," Al said slowly. "I am surprised at, I thought Harry wasn't into that."

"Strange choice of words, Al," Tim laughed.

After a pause, Al also laughed, "Yeah."

"I never thought infidelity was funny," John sighed.

39

"You're a real bowl of mush," Billy chided. "All's we're doin' is havin' some fun." He paused, looking back at Al. "Kelly caught them goin' at it last week."

"What did Harry do?" Tim asked.

"Kelly said 'ol Harry gave her ten hours overtime for keepin' her mouth shut."

"She didn't keep her mouth shut if she told you," Al observed.

"No, but she still got the ten extra hours in her last pay check," Billy persisted. "And Harry's still bangin' good 'ol Ann."

"Maybe she's not gettin' any from her old man, you guess?" Tim asked.

"I don't know, but Ann's been after anythin' she can get for a long time," Billy said. "You know, she ain't half bad for an old woman."

"What does that mean?" John asked.

"It don't mean nothin'," Billy said loudly. "It means I don't think she looks half bad for a fifty year old woman."

"You gonna try?" Al patted Billy's shoulder.

Billy remained silent for a short while, then shook his head. "Naw."

"Are there any other bulletins from work?" John asked.

"Since you asked," Al answered. "Did you hear about Harry?"

"The one who's using Ann?" John asked.

"I don't know who's usin' who," Al said. "But, Harry's in a heap of trouble."

"What'd he do now?" Billy asked. "Not that I've got no sympathy for that scum bag."

"His house is bein' repossessed, and the company's not too happy 'bout that."

"How did you find out?" Tim asked.

"His name's in the paper, I saw it in the legal adds last week; the house goes on the block the first Monday of next month."

"Did you know his wife left him?" Tim asked.

40

"No," Billy replied.

"I'd heard that, but he ain't said nothin' to me," Al said.

"I don't think it would concern you," John said.

"Yeah, but how come Tim knows?" Al insisted.

"I overheard him on the phone with his wife's lawyer," Tim paused. "And it sounded like she was takin' him for everythin' he owns."

"That still don't say why he's bangin' Ann," Billy observed.

"It could be that they're both lonely," John concluded.

"Maybe," Tim said. "But, I never did like Harry's wife none. I mean, at the Christmas party, or at the Summer picnic, she'd be so damned uppity. It was like we all was the scum of the earth or somethin'."

"Yeah," Al chimed in. "You put your finger on it all right. I knew I didn't like her, but I never thought 'bout why, and you've said it."

"Why are people that way?" Billy asked. "Some people think they're so much better than everyone else." He glared at John.

"And some people are," John calmly replied.

"You always think you're such a big shit," Billy grumbled.

"No, I'm no better than you, but I'm also no worse than you," John said.

"Yeah." Billy turned his eyes to the front windshield, not wanting to continue this verbal swordfight.

"Harry's wife always talked down to all of us, even you, John," Al said.

"She's still living in the old South, and she's the real white woman," John chuckled.

"So?" Billy said abruptly. "We's all white, as white as her."

"We get our hands dirty doin' work, so we ain't as white as she is," Al said. "I see what John's talkin' 'bout."

41

"Yeah," Tim added. "Harry's better off gettin' rid of her anyway."

"Amen to that," Billy said. "But I still think Harry's a son of a bitch."

"What for?" Tim asked.

"He's never goin' to bat for none of us with the higher ups," Billy said, nodding his head for emphasis.

"Like how?" Al asked.

"Like never givin' us no overtime when we need it, especially around Christmas," Billy answered.

"That may be out of his hands, Billy," John said.

"How come he can give Kelly ten hours of it for keepin' her mouth shut?" Billy asked indignantly.

"You've got a point," John admitted.

"Ten hours ain't much," Tim said. "Besides, he does give us all overtime once in a while."

"But," Billy continued. "I've tried to get transferred to maintenance for two years, and he's always blocked it."

"We know, but you ain't that good for maintenance," Tim quietly said.

"What does that mean," Billy demanded.

"Never mind," Tim quickly said. "I didn't say nothin'."

"I don't got no use for the man," Billy stated.

The sky became darker, making the late afternoon feel to the senses as dusk. Small spots of water splattered on the front windshield of the van.

"Look at that stuff," Tim said.

"Is that rain, or snow?" John asked.

"Looks like rain to me," Billy answered.

"No." Tim nodded towards the front hood. "Look at it bouncin' off the front hood, I think it's sleet."

"Shit," Al said loudly. "That's all we need."

"Don't make no difference to me," Tim said. "I'm still goin' hunting this week no matter what the weather's like."

"Me too," Billy said. "No matter what."

Al looked at John, who nodded. "We're in agreement so drive on, Tim my man."

Over the next fifteen minutes, the rain and sleet turned to sleet and snow. An ice glaze grew over most of the small vegetation along the road, although the asphalt road surface was still only wet.

"There's the forest service road." Tim pointed towards a large, spreading oak tree, sticking its ponderous branches out of a stand of twenty year old pine trees.

A wide rutted dirt entrance into the forest opened onto the blacktop like a worn out funnel. A white frosting was visible in the bottoms of old tire ruts in the dirt road.

"We've only got another ten minutes or so," John said. "Be real careful on the flat stones after the creek crossing."

"Yeah, I was thinking about that." Tim slowly turned the van onto the dirt road, straddling two deep tire impressions, and driving slowly into the gray, cold and wet forest.

Tim guided the large van carefully down the time-worn dirt road. The squashing noise from the shocks as they attempted to stabilize the van were as loud as the crunching of tires against gravel and partially frozen mud.

The sleet and snow turned into snow, then the fine mist of small snow flakes turned into a white fog of medium sized snow flakes.

"Get us there in one piece," Al said with a nervous laugh.

"That's not as funny as you think," Tim said. "The van's slidin' all over the place, and I'm barely movin' now."

"I think the turn off to the ridge's up there." Billy pointed in front of him.

"Yeah," Tim said. "There's the crossing."

A crudely constructed bridge, made out of four telephone poles and many large planks, lay ahead of the van across a small creek.

"Take it real slow," John softly said.

"You got it." Tim moved the van onto, then across the bridge at a crawling speed.

43

"I'm going straight for the site right next to the creek." Tim sighed. "I know it's further, but I ain't goin' up and down that steep hill to get to the other one.

"I ain't seen no one else, have any of you?" Billy asked.

"Not a soul," Al answered.

"Maybe we're the only ones stupid enough to come out here in weather like this," Tim laughed.

"We ain't got far to go now, don't stop 'cause it might be hard to get goin' again," Billy commented, pointing to the road ahead of them which now was completely white.

"Shit, Look at it snow out there," Al said. "First thing I'm gonna do is get a fire goin' and get warm, then try to stay warm."

After five nervous minutes of watching each inch of white ground the van passed over, Al looked out his side window.

"Look at that," Al observed, "They must of clear cut a big chunk of land, look at that."

Ahead of them, a vast area of land opened up. Irregular piles of bulldozed hardwoods and pine stumps littered the clear cut land, which gently sloped down to a thick border of uncut forest.

"That must be the woods next to the creek, way down there." John strained to see the scene in the failing light and the heavy snow storm.

"Yeah, I think it is." Tim looked in the direction of the dark tree line.

The van jerked suddenly into a deep rut on what must have been the edge of the dirt road. Yanking the steering wheel in the opposite direction, Tim tried to steer back on to the center of the road.

"Don't over steer," Al shouted

The van continued to gather speed as it drifted down the gentle hill, more or less following the path of the road. Part way down the snow covered road, it turned three hundred and sixty degrees. By this time, each man had gripped seats, handles, anything stationary.

Moving forty miles an hour, the van turned sideways again, struck a rock, then fell on its side. An ice chest rapidly shot forward and struck Al on the side of his head, then landed on John's ribs. The van toppled over, Tim and John smashed into the side of the van as it slid along the ground. Billy fell onto Tim's side, as Al's unconscious body fell across John.

The van slid off the road path. It clipped a pine tree, the center of its roof crashed against a large red oak. With this final blow, all four of the men smashed into the crumpling van roof. As the echoing sounds of the crash died, the van lay on its side, silent. The four men inside it also lay silent, but alive.

Chapter 3

Cradled in Mary's arms, a small pink wrinkled ten week old white boy slept soundly. Her husband John sat glumly nearby. A single flickering oil lamp lit the small room at eight o'clock that evening. Their conversation over possible futures grew as dark as the night outside.

Mary was a light complexioned black woman in her late twenties. She was short and quite thin. John Burns was slightly under six feet tall with well defined muscles from years of hard work. His complexion was slightly darker than Mary's, but his facial features were distinctly Caucasian and his eyes were blue-green.

"She's callin' him Paul," she told her future husband wistfully. She looked north, into the dark trees outside their window. "I grew up in that house, it's a grand house with many fine things in it; I once thought distinguished people lived in it too."

46

Mary's father was first cousin of her former owner, Sarah Bellows. Sarah's family had once owned both Mary and John, although they were now legally free. They had once been house slaves, but John Burns had worked in the fields for the last five years, mainly due to his argumentative personality.

His right hand paused on his bristly chin as he fell into a thoughtful pause. "I don't know about that child."

Unable to sit still, he began to pace. His boots made a hollow thump as each fell on the poorly spaced boards of the two room shack

Three generations before, the Bellows family had started this plantation in 1789; handing down to their descendents not only the land and slaves, but also a fear of rebellion. The patriarch Bellows, in addition to owning lands in Virginia and Georgia, owned a half interest in two sugar plantations in Haiti until the slave rebellion of 1791 pushed him to near ruin. Even though his savage mistreatment of his slaves stemmed more from a fear of failure than sheer cruelty, Bellows' descendants unbridled savagery towards slaves gradually became habitual, automatic. In 1818 the family consolidated their debts, sold their remaining land in Virginia and moved to Georgia where they began construction of a grand house, with a great columned porch on three sides.

Benjamin Bellows, Sarah's father, formed a company of soldiers within three months of the Fort Sumter incident. After a year of undistinguished service, his company joined the Confederate Army of Northern Virginia in 1862. One year after Sarah's mother died of pneumonia, Benjamin died in the battle of Seven Pines on June 1, 1862. His death left Sarah alone to manage the large plantation. Three years later, she was inconveniently pregnant.

Sarah Bellows was only one year older than Mary Smith; the two girls had grown up together. When Mary was about twelve, she became Sarah's personal slave. Over the years, the imposed social order drew the former friends into the formal relationship of master and slave. Sarah's father forced Mary and

47

other female slaves to have children so he could sell them for cash. Mary was forcibly bred twice, once as she turned thirteen, and again when she was fifteen; both of her children sold at auction when they reached the age of five.

In the small dark room, holding Sarah's baby Mary watched John, who had stopped pacing. "She ain't going to take this boy, and nobody else will neither." She held his glance for a silent moment, then dropped her eyes to watch the sleeping baby. "He's one of God's creatures and that crazy woman in the big white house means him harm if no one takes him."

"And, that's supposed to be that?" John stopped pacing as he stared down at Mary. "You and me gonna live together, ain't I got no say?"

"John Burns, of course you got your say. We've got to get this straight between us."

"I'll say," John answered. She ignored him.

"This baby ain't yours, and it ain't mine. You know I can't have no babies since I got the fever, everybody else on this plantation knows it too. I don't see nothin' wrong with starting out our lives together with a pretty baby boy like this since I ain't gonna get no more of my own. I can't get no word about my boys, I had someone write the government to help me find them, but I don't hold no hope out. Least the white man can't sell our babies off no more." She shifted the baby around in her lap to show his face more plainly to John. "Besides he's some of my blood too, you know that to be true."

"Yes. But he ain't one of us."

"I think that's why she sent for me to come down to Savannah and bring her baby back," Mary said. "No one knew Miss Sarah was with child when she left, I still can't believe it myself."

"I don't care 'bout none of that," John said. "This is 'bout us, not that white baby boy, he don't belong to us no way."

"You and me don't belong to nobody either," Mary's voice lowered. "Your daddy was some mean cracker and my daddy was Miss Sarah's cousin."

"And this is Miss Sarah's child, ain't nothin' but the bastard son of that cracker up there in the big house." John raised his voice, the baby woke.

The child gurgled loudly, annoyed at being torn from a dream and beginning to breathe noisily as he wondered if he should be fed or not. Mary rocked him in her arms until he closed his eyes again.

"You keep your voice down," she scolded in a whisper. "I want to finish talkin' with you before I have to take him next door to Miss Sally's for feedin'."

"Ain't no business of mine, woman." John shook his head slowly. Then he glared at Mary, looking straight into her eyes. "She feeds and clothes us better than most, but that's only 'cause we used to be her house niggers. I belonged to that woman up there like a horse or a cow, and ain't nothin' you can say's going to make me take care of her damned baby 'cause I feel owned enough for three life times already."

"It was that Yankee captain who stayed here last Spring, he took a liking to Miss Sarah." Mary shook her head. "He hid in her room one night and talked her out of her womanhood; Miss Sarah said he didn't ask, he took, but I think different. Miss Sarah said he told her he loved her but he left and I don't guess we'll ever see him again no way."

"That ain't our doin'. All of them white men do that to our women folk whenever they want, so if they do it to each other, they should keep their own damned babies and not give them to us, another mouth to feed and less for ourselves."

"That woman wants to throw this baby out like it was a piece of leftover chicken. She never laid eyes on him, that makes it better in her mind, but he's still garbage to her," Mary quieted her voice. "I know what she's doin' ain't right, but Miss Sarah was taken, and no woman deserves that."

"Woman." John stood over Mary. "Your mama was raped, and my mama was raped. Those fine white folk dumped us in the fields to fend for ourselves, does that make this right?"

49

"Miss Sarah ain't like her father," Mary pleaded. "I grew up with that woman, and she ain't no monster, least ways she don't mean to be."

"The war's over, and her father's dead, I still praise God for that," John said. "She could accept losin' the war by lettin' us go, or givin' us some land to work for ourselves, but, no, she ain't got no plans for that; she's gonna work us like slaves."

"I know she ain't got that meanness in her like her father," Mary repeated.

She ain't?" John asked. "Then, why'd she tell you she'd kill her own child?"

Mary didn't answer.

"I'll tell you why, she's crazy," John said. "Could be 'cause she lost her daddy and most all her kin, or maybe it's 'cause she's all alone on this big plantation and at the mercy of them carpetbaggers."

"I don't want him dumped in the woods like trash, even this baby don't deserve that," she replied. "He sure ain't going to live up at the big house like he should."

"He sure looks like he belongs up at the big house, he's the whitest boy I've ever seen." John took a long look at the baby.

Mary followed his glance. "Nobody'll claim him, but he belongs here all the same. His real mama owns all this land and yet he'll still work it 'till he dies, like us."

"That ain't got nothin' to do with nothin'." John shook his head. "So the white folks up are goin' to work him to death like they're goin' to work us to death, that don't mean we should feed him our food, wrap him in our clothes."

"Miss Sarah Bellows is marrying Mr. Appleby in a few months, soon as he gets back from Richmond. He's pure mean and he don't know about her bein' pregnant by that Yankee, or that I got the baby. Miss Sarah needs to marry him so she'll have a man to run this place and we need to keep her secret so we'll get what she promised me today."

John focused on Mary's face. "What you say?"

50

"She told me today that the only way this baby will live is for me to raise him. What with the war ended, there's too many babies left alone so this boy could have been give up by any mulatto; no one would think much about it, let alone guess it's really Miss Sarah's baby."

"I don't believe it, everybody knows it's hers; within a year, everyone who's from here will know that white woman in the big house had a baby." John looked hard into Mary's eyes. "He's too white. It's in his blood, he'll turn on us in the end anyway."

"She went away to Savannah as soon as she knew she was with child, she told everybody that her daddy's lawyer sent her a message to meet him there; something about the plantation," Mary insisted. "As far as I know, nobody from here knows any other reason why she left, and Ms. Sarah wants to keep it that way."

"Most folks around here will know it soon enough," John disagreed. "Secrets ain't too well kept around this place."

"She give the boy fifty acres of his own when she dies, maybe sooner; she's givin' him the fifty acres down by the creek, where it crosses the road close to town." Mary rocked the baby. "She says that we all belong to this land, and she wants the baby to have a part of it. She can't raise him, but she wants me to raise him for her."

John stopped pacing and sat in a chair facing Mary and the baby.

"I ain't sayin' I'll change my mind, but what else she tell you that you ain't told me?"

"She wants us to raise him for her, she ain't never going to claim him, she can't," Mary continued. "She said she knows that her and me are cousins, she heard her father jokin' about it before the war. So at least this way the baby would stay in her blood family."

John looked hard at the woman sitting in front of him. "Fifty acres, we get it when she's dead? Hell, woman, she's as old

51

as we is, she'll outlive us by years." He paused to think. "She's so cussed mean, she'll outlive her own child."

"She ain't as mean as the man she's marrying, besides she said she'd give the land to the baby when he gets twelve years, or if she dies, whatever comes first."

"Hell, woman, why didn't you say that to start with." John resumed pacing. "I could use an extra boy to work those fifty acres. It'd be good bossin' massa's kid for a change."

"He's going to be your boy, not none of the white folks', you remember that," Mary spoke carefully. "If you spread any of who he is around, everything'll be taken away from us, and Miss Sarah's new husband'll probably have us both done in."

John thought for a second, looked down at Mary and the baby, and spoke softly, "You like that baby?"

"I was waitin' for you to ask." Mary beamed at the tall man next to her. "Yes, I like this baby a heap more than Miss Sarah does. She ain't never touched him since she birthed him; I've been his mama since that day, and I do like him enough to raise him on those fifty acres."

"I like you enough, woman, and I guess that baby, and that fifty acres, could be ours."

Chapter 4

Trust not the horse, O Trojans. Be it what it may, I fear the Grecians even when they offer gifts.
Virgil, Aeneid, bk. 2.

East of the grand Bellows-Appleby home, a fifteen minute walk, but not within sight, lay a collection of twenty seven dilapidated homes surrounding a communal well. Walking past the well, a plump fitly dressed lawyer in his early thirties moved cautiously. The clapboard buildings had once contained slaves. Now called tenant farmers, they all still lived here. The lawyer glanced with a nervous smile at several older black men leaning against the edge of one of the old houses. The bright morning sun washed the black men's tattered clothes as they watched him pause, then nod, walking more surely to one house. Tugging at the sleeves of his long business coat, he stopped in front of a weathered gray door which lay open. A small boy peered out. Casting a large shadow over the boy, the man hesitated for a second.

"Is your mama at home?"

The five year old stared up at the stranger. The man noted the child's light brown, fine hair, and the freckles under the dirt that covered his face.

"Is your mama here, boy?" he repeated.

At that moment, Mary reached the sill. The boy darted out the door into the open dirt area around the cluster of houses. A small trail of dust followed him as he spun to his left and headed towards a stand of new pine trees, never saying a word.

Mary had gained a layer of muscles since leaving the main house and returning to the fields with her husband. Her face had settled into an expression which had lost much of its former fire.

She took in a shallow breath, "Can I help you, sir?"

"Yes." The large man clasped his hands behind him. "If your name is Mary Burns, I need to talk to you."

"That's me." She looked apprehensive. "Has somethin' happened?"

"No. My name is Mr. William Jenkins, I'm a lawyer from back in town."

Mary stepped out of the house to the few boards propped up by rocks which served as a front porch. "My man's not here now, you might want to come back in a bit."

"No, I need to talk to you, I have something for you."

"What?" An expression of dread flicked across her face.

"Mrs. Sarah Bellows Appleby died a few months ago," Jenkins began.

"I know, we all went to the funeral; us folks had to stand back so far we almost didn't hear nothin', but I went," Mary replied.

"I know, I was there also, and I saw you and your husband but I didn't see your son."

"Didn't want him to go, I had my reasons," Mary said slowly.

"That doesn't concern me," The lawyer said. "I have some legal papers for you to put your mark to."

"What papers?"

"Mrs. Appleby had named this family in her will. Although I did not draw up this will, I was Mrs. Appleby's lawyer when it was probated. Her husband's lawyer contested this passage in the will, but the judge ruled for me, which led me to seek you here." Jenkins took in a deep breath. "The contested clause concerns fifty acres."

The full implications of that court battle passed through Jenkins' thoughts, though he would never speak them. Sarah Bellows' father had some influential friends before the war, and

54

one of them was now the local judge. The Bellows' family friends all agreed that Sarah may have been murdered by her husband, know for his ruthlessness. They also knew Sarah had been considering leaving her abusive husband as soon as she could arrange the legal documents. First she planned to wrest her land holdings and cash away back under her control. This last small bequest from Sarah to her former slave was allowed by the court as much as a slight to Joshua Appleby as a kindness to the Bellows family.

"My land?" Mary interrupted. "So she remembered, God bless her."

"I see you know what this is about." The lawyer's posture relaxed for the first time.

"Miss Sarah promised this to me before she ever got married, she liked me a lot then, and she promised it to me for my son, Paul."

"That is exactly what her will said that was drawn up before she got married." Jenkins paused to consider the gravity of the whole situation, then continued. "Your son has the land; you and your husband will keep title to it until he reaches twenty one years, then it will pass to him."

"That's what she promised." Mary clasped her hands together and grinned almost to tears. "God bless her."

"Yes, well." The lawyer shifted nervously from one foot to the other. "All I need for you to do is put your mark on this paper."

He pulled a long legal document from the inside pocked of his perspiration stained coat and held it up to her.

"And, I shall file it in the Clerk's office for you, then that will be that," Jenkins added.

Mary almost grabbed the paper and the pen he had inked for her and placed a large X over the line at the bottom.

"Is that all right?" She asked.

The lawyer looked at the document and signed his name next to the X, then he blew on the ink for a moment and held the document out in the still damp air.

"That will do fine."

"How much we owe you? I'll pay what it takes to do this right," Mary eagerly said.

"The estate paid all costs, you have nothing to do but move on the fifty acres." Jenkins folded the paper and placed it in his coat pocket.

"Miss Sarah paid for it all?" Mary looked astounded.

"His wife's last will and testament astonished Mr. Appleby; many things in it did not sit well with him." The lawyer sounded slightly guilty, he had not meant to speak openly about the powerful land owner.

"Don't surprise me none," Mary retorted. "That man's pure mean, and even Miss Sarah saw that in him last year; we knew, we all knew long before she did."

"Well," William said, more nervous. "I must get back to town before the courthouse closes."

He tilted his head towards Mary and turned to leave, then stopped for a second. He looked thoughtful and spoke carefully. "If you ever want to sell that small parcel of land, please contact me first."

"I ain't never going to sell that land, mister." Mary still had a broad grin on her face. "Never."

"Well, if you change your mind, let me know first."

Chapter 5

In spite of her best efforts, Mary never located her two sons after they were sold to a plantation in north Florida. She arranged a special place in her heart for Paul, loving him almost as much as she could love a natural child. To his own surprise, John took the small white boy under his wing and took pride in Paul's everyday achievements; he taught Paul all that he knew of farming, and about staying safe in the community. In 1874, in the deep South, the climate for any person of black, mixed, Republican or Yankee blood was hazardous. Since they themselves were of mixed blood, the Burns assumed everyone thought their son, Paul, was from the same lineage, even though his features were all too white. Paul's mannerisms were the same as his adoptive parents; his fear of the Southern white man was also the same as his parents. Although many people in both societies knew who Paul's real mother was, no one spoke of it.

Their small parcel of land meant more to them than the tens of thousands of acres meant to the new generation of white plantation owners. Some former slaves were given forty acres by the occupying Union governments, but not in this county; a gift of land to a non-white was unheard of in this corner of the South. Their fifty acres made Mary and John feel even more a

57

part of the land, they now owned what once had owned them. A strong, uncut stand of hardwoods lined Walton creek, providing shade for their dirt floored farm house. Several years passed as the family farmed peaceably, growing even closer to the land.

The Burns worked their farm for only three years before a group of white riders armed with long muskets and cap and ball revolvers demanded they vacate their home. The fifty acres must be given back to the rightful owner, the eldest son of Joshua Appleby.

Joshua Appleby had two sons from a previous marriage before he met Sarah. Sarah Bellows Appleby had contacted a lawyer she knew in Atlanta to draw up a new will, one which would specifically disinherit her husband and his children. She died three weeks after contacting the lawyer and before she signed the new will. Although her death was suspicious, the sheriff found no direct evidence which called for an investigation. Joshua felt that his second deceased wife's property was all his now, a legacy to hand down to his sons. To this end the Burns family would be killed if necessary to clear the land for the plantation. The Burns' small plot was key to making up the full five thousand acre holding Joshua was to give his son. Their fifty acres lay three miles from the small growing town. The land was flat and mostly cleared except for a thick wood near the creek which ran through the back third of the property. As land, it was a prime property because it joined another large plantation with the Appleby holdings. More importantly, it also lay on both sides of the main road into the growing town.

Mary and her husband were silent in the face of the armed men, but as soon as the band of men delivered their belligerent message and rode back in the direction of the large plantation, John Burns spun angrily on his feet to face his wife.

"We ain't quite white 'nough for them folks, is we?" He demanded.

"We've got the legal document, signed by Miss Sarah; I've got it hid back in the house, and we're goin' right to the lawyer in town tomorrow and make damn sure we don't lose this land."

"You see your lawyer if you want to, but I'm gonna get some guns and some men together and see to it they don't come back here no more," John stammered.

"All you'll do is get yourself hung on some tree up on plantation land, and Paul and me'll never hear nothin' more 'bout you," Mary declared. "Besides, you know damn well who Paul's real mama was anyway; I saved proof of that too, and I even hid it from you. If they try anythin' too crooked with us, I'll get the whole damn plantation for Paul, and where do you think that'll put those white bastards up there."

John looked askance at his wife. "You know where somethin' like that'll get all us for sure, woman, it'll get us dead so don't you even think about it."

"I'll be thinkin' anythin' I want to when you start hollerin' like you are now 'bout killin' white men," Mary said. "You is all I got in this world, man, and I ain't gonna lose you yet."

"I guess you're right this time." John calmed a bit. "We've got the title to this land all legal so if they want it, they'll have to pay for it at least."

"That's better," Mary said, "Let's get to town and see that lawyer who did the papers for us when the will was read."

Paul remained at the farm with a teenage girl who was related to John while his parents hitched the two horses to the large wagon and guided the beasts toward town. The ride was a short one, less than one hour to the small town which served the four large plantations surrounding it. There was only one road through the community with many side streets jutting off it once the wooden sidewalks began lining the main road.

As agriculture flourished in the Reconstruction South, this town had bulged with new feed stores, blacksmiths, banks, general stores, lawyers, doctors, veterinarians and any business which supported the new found wealth. Home construction was heading from the northern limit of the town out in Mary and John Burns's direction.

John stopped the wagon in front of the lawyer's office; Mary got off to wait for the lawyer while John went to buy some staples from the only store which would sell goods to non-whites, through the back door. When he finished, he drove their wagon back to the lawyer's office, only to find Mary still waiting for the lawyer to return.

"Where is he?" John sat in the straight backed wooden chair next to her.

"He says he won't talk to a woman 'bout nothin' important 'lest her husband's in the same room with her."

"Shit."

"Don't get too hot 'bout it, you're here now anyway."

"Well." John let out a big breath. "Where is he?"

"He went to get a haircut while you was at the store."

"How long ago?" The anger in John's voice rose again.

"'Bout twenty five minutes ago, he should be back any minute."

A large, fat balding man in his forties walked through the door, carefully shutting it behind him.

"I thought it might be you hitching the wagon in front of my place." William Jenkins removed his dark, blocked hat and placed it slowly on a hat rack near the door. His voice was quiet, evasive and professional. He looked away from John's stare and walked to a small desk next to a door which led into his private office.

"What exactly can I do for you?" He asked in a brusque voice, managing to barely move his mustache.

"You can help us keep the land you gave us title to after Mrs. Appleby died," Mary blurted out.

"Now, wait a minute." The lawyer's right eye twitched. "I did not give you title to any property; that property you've built on was part of a settlement of the Bellows-Appleby estate, and you know that Sarah's husband protested her gift to you in the will at the time."

60

"He can protest all he wants to, but Miss Sarah gave me that land, and you know damn well why she did." Mary rose slightly from the hard chair.

"Calm down, woman." John put his right hand on his wife's shoulder. "Mr. Lawyer, all we want is what's ours, and to be left alone, it ain't much land no way."

"I know, Mr. Burns, it doesn't seem like that much next to the thousands of acres held by the few families around here, but, well, Mr. Appleby still insists it's his land, not yours. He insists that his wife owned both of you, and that no horse, pig, or no nigger's ever going to own land, especially his land."

John cocked his head to one side and stared straight into the lawyer's face. "Jest what you sayin'?"

The stout man behind the desk shifted in his chair and stared straight into the desk top.

"What I need to say is, that, well, Mr. Appleby usually gets his way, and, well, he obtained title to your land not five days ago," he said.

"How'd he do that?" Mary half stood from the chair again.

John put his hand on his wife's shoulder and gently pushed her back down.

"We would like to know how even he can steal land from simple folks like us?" John asked.

The lawyer leaned forward in his chair, and placed his face between his hands, slowly pulling it back out.

"Look, I'll be straight with the two of you, a lot of people in this county think you folks are niggers, I never did, but a lot do. All they want is to see you folks leaving this county, and off the land they think should never belong to any of you." The lawyer sounded sad.

John and Mary both sank a little lower into their chair.

"Yes, legally Mr. Appleby stole your land from you, but he owns most of the politicians and judges in this part of the state and he can do anything he wants to, and there's nothing even I could do to stop him. With the Yankees and the

61

Republicans gone from this state, there's no more can be done for you people that way."

"I know a way to stop him, cold." Mary leaned forward in her seat.

"If you mean Sarah's bastard child, your son Paul, that doesn't mean a thing. This is a small county and no secrets exist between any of the old white families living here. Sarah told her husband about the child before her death; she wanted him to raise Paul in the plantation, but Joshua Appleby became enraged. He beat her up, right there in her bedroom. Some say that killed her, some say she was sick and half dead already, I don't know, but I do know he hates free niggers, and he hates you two even more for raising his wife's bastard child." The lawyer took a deep breath and continued. "Take my advice and quietly get out of that farm tomorrow, and at least the three of you will be alive because he'll send his riders as sure as the sun comes up, and they'll make short work of hanging all three of you."

There was a full two minutes of silence in the room; the steady click of a small clock pendulum was the only sound.

"Where?" Mary weakly broke the silence. "Where do we go?"

"I've been thinking about that. I saw you driving up my office, and I went out to talk to some folks, not get a haircut like I told you."

"Well?" John looked crossly at Jenkins. "You sayin' we're still slaves, where you got for us to go? Can't get to no Yankee state without a stake, not with a family least ways, don't know nobody up there anyways."

"Please understand." The lawyer tiredly shook his head. "I do sympathize with you, but I have to live and make a living in this community, and I can't do either if Joshua Appleby takes a dislike to me because of something I do for you."

"We've all gotta live somewhere, mister, lest we don't live at all." John looked at the lawyer, who remained silent. "I live on the land near where my white daddy owned, and my black mama died on, and no matter where they shove me, that's the land I'm gonna be on."

"Well," Mary said, looking from one man to the other. "Where do we go?"

"There's a large farm way out in the woods, called the Rose Community. It was run by some religious folks before the War; who didn't believe in slaves, but they were quiet about it. It's now run by the people who live there, all of them together. Some religious people live there still, they're white, but most are free mulattos like you two; you'd be welcome there, and I've sent word that you're coming."

"What 'bout Paul?" Mary asked.

"He's your son, no one else's. Keep all the papers you have proving he's white, times may change for him."

"Where's this place?" John asked.

"Follow the river up stream about twenty miles, take the ferry crossing at the Rose Community Road and there it is."

John turned to his wife. "Woman, that's land my grandma died on; the white man she was sold to owned that land."

Chapter 6

The snow falls harder as the push of bitter wind from the northwest is a steady fifteen miles per hour, gusting much higher. The scene of the wrecked van is invisible through the white curtain from any distance greater than one hundred yards. The slide path left by the wrecked van becomes covered quickly with new fallen white snow, the relentless snowfall covers the whole scene; there will soon be no trace of the van's intrusion into the forest.

An intense odor of raw gasoline lingers between strong gusts of wind, the tank in the rear of the van drips fuel slowly from a narrow one inch rupture; it's a small tear in the metal, but gasoline is steadily leaking from it.

An undetermined amount of time passes before a sound comes from the wreck.

Sharp cracking sounds break the silence, coming from under the crumpled hood. The severed positive starter cable leading from the battery falls to make contact with the still grounded oil pan. The gusts of wind catch the thick wire and slap it against the flat metal, making a large spark each time.

64

A groan comes from within the overturned van, the moan is low at first, then increases to form a word.

"Jesus!" The voice pauses, then rises again. "Jesus!"

John tries to raise his arm as the voice again rises in front of him.

"Jesus, help me!" Billy shouts.

"Can you move?" John asks while pushing the large cooler off his ribcage.

"God," Billy pleads.

"Shut up and try to move." John pulls himself from under Al, who is still motionless.

John sniffs the air. "Shit, smell that, gas!"

"Oh God," Billy moans. "I pray to You, don't let me die."

John pulls himself to the side door facing the gray, white sky, he then pulls the handle and pushes the door open. Snow falls into the cool interior, melting slowly on the men inside. John looks down at Billy, who begins to weep.

"Can you move?" John asks in a firm voice.

"I think so." Billy grabs onto the seat back and pulls himself off Tim.

"Good, then, pull Tim out of here, and I'll get Al. Stay calm, but there's gas all over the place so we'd better get the others far away from here, fast."

"Oh God, please don't let me die!" Billy looks up, past John.

"I don't think God is going to do everything for you right now," John says loudly. "Get your act together, stop praying for divine intervention and get the hell out here with Tim."

"Yeah, yeah." Billy grabs Tim in rapid, nervous moves and tries to lift him to the still closed door, facing up.

"Be careful." John slowly pulls Al onto the cold exterior of the van. "He may have neck injuries, or a broken back so be careful."

Both men hear a sharp crack.

"Oh lord, what's that!" Billy demands.

"It sounds like an electrical spark," John says slowly.

Another crack shoots into the forest, then two more.

"God, it'll set off the gas," Billy shouts.

"Please shut up, we have to get our friends out of here fast so help me and don't worry about the gas; calm down and work carefully but fast, all right?"

John busies himself with extracting Al from the wreck.

"All right," Billy responds.

Billy quietly climbs out of the now open door and slowly pulls Tim out. John jumps to the ground and motions to Billy to help him bring down the two other men, one at a time. John and Billy carry each unconscious man; Billy holds their feet, and John uses his hands under their arms to support their heads. They carry their friends gingerly to a small cluster of oak trees fifty yards away. As they set Al slowly to the ground, John looks at the van.

"We've got to get as much out of there as we can, let's go," John insists.

Billy stares at the white ground before he answers, "I don't know, it could go off any minute."

"Look, how the hell are we supposed to stay alive out here with no food, no dry cloths, no tent?" John demands.

Billy looks back up at John, his eyes dart between the up turned van and John as he answers, "Let's go, but don't take forever."

The two men rush to the van and pull open one rear door; John pushes his way into the cluttered interior and begins to throw things out the open door. He grabs three duffel bags of clothes, four rifles, four backpacks and one cooler of food and throws them onto the ground.

"You drag them far enough away from the van so a fire can't get to them," John shouts from within the vehicle.

Billy does not answer, he starts to pull each item fifty feet from the van, in the direction of the two unconscious men.

John grabs a large tent and throws it out the open door, then he throws the long sack of aluminum tent poles out after it,

66

then he grabs the camp stove and one cylinder of propane and throws it out the door.

A loud electrical crack thunders, then a soft sound follows, like air rushing into a vacuum.

"Get the hell outta there!" Billy shouts.

John sees a bright orange flame through the front windshield, partially covered with snow. A gust of wind cuts the top of the flame spear from its base; it hangs in mid air, then extinguishes. John grabs two sacks and dives out the rear door, rolling on the cold, hard ground. He feels the intense heat of the flame as it follows the path the gasoline left on and beneath the snow cover. John rolls again and again, trying to hang onto the bundles he carries with him.

Billy runs towards their companions under the leafless trees as John stops rolling and looks towards the van.

Surrounding the van is a large multi-spiked jungle of flames; first a loud hissing sound escapes, then a deafening roar. Four separate explosions punctuate the scene as the remaining canisters of propane blow up. The flames become red, blue and orange, they speed toward the top of the tree the van is wrapped around, then die back down. The now fully ruptured gas tank explodes. A loud boom echoes through the woods as the van is torn into many large and small pieces, each of them landing with a soft thump at different times. A blackened, warped hull of Tim's van lays on the snowfield, next to the tall oak.

The snow still falls, the wind blows from the Northwest, and the crisp, fresh smelling forest becomes silent again.

John, putting his hands on his hips, looks at the burning hull of what used to be Tim's van while Billy, holding a large duffel bag, walks slowly to the stand of oaks and their unconscious friends.

John walks to the pile of materials in the snow, picks several up and carries them to where Al and Tim lay.

Chapter 7

Patience and tenacity of purpose are worth more than twice their weight of cleverness.

Thomas Henry, Collected Essays, vol. 3, 1893.

The wind and snow combined into a single adversary as it closed in on the four men huddled inside all the warm clothes they could wear.

The flames and smoke from the wrecked van had disappeared after almost an hour. Tim had a little over a quarter of a tank of gas in his van to feed the flames when the van slid into the tree. Only a blank white countryside was now visible; the area immediately surrounding the small cluster of oaks was almost devoid of trees. The only tree in sight was the one the van had struck; no tree line was visible through the storm and the road they had been on was no longer discernible.

Al came back to reality first. An hour later, Tim focused on the scene.

"What happened?" Tim pulled his coat tighter around his neck.

"The van's dead, but none of us are." John forced a grin. "How do you feel, does anything feel broken?"

"I feel awful sore, but." Tim sat up and slowly moved his arms and legs; he wiggled his fingers, staring at them as he did. "Nothin's broken."

"Try to get up and move around a bit," John sounded concerned about his friend. "You've been out longer than the rest of us."

Tim rose to his feet and leaned against a tree.

"My head hurts like hell, I musta hit somethin'. Where's the van?" His forehead wrinkled and his eyes took on a bewildered look.

"It's over there," Billy answered, pointing into the dense white storm.

"Where?" Tim strained his eyes in the direction Billy's finger was pointing.

Al walked closer to Tim and answered, "It blew up, you ain't never gonna find all of it." Al slapped his gloved hands together as if he were playing the cymbals in a large orchestra.

"Shit," Tim whispered. "It ain't even paid for."

"It is now." Billy looked into the snow storm. "I ain't never seen it snow this hard before."

"Me neither," Al added. "What the hell's goin' on?"

"This is what a blizzard looks like," John replied. "I've been in several back in New England."

"That don't make no sense," Tim sounded confused. "The weather man on channel five didn't say nothin' about no snow storm."

"Like that fag knows his ass from a hole in the ground," Billy chuckled.

"Least ways he knows if it's gonna snow or not," Tim retorted.

"It could be a fast moving storm that went out to the coast instead of up the mountains," Al chimed in. "That's how we get snow around here."

"It could be," John sounded skeptical. "I checked the computer for the weather maps before I left and there wasn't anything big enough for a storm like this."

"The computer don't know shit neither," Billy huffed.

Tim turned to Billy and shrugged his shoulders. "Well, it's snowing like a son of a bitch now, so what're we gonna do?"

69

"Hell," Billy answered Tim. "You only lost your damned van, I had a much worse time of it."

Tim remained silent, but glared a question at Billy.

"Shit, I swallowed a whole chew of tobacco and I'm sick as a dog 'cause of your damned drivin'," Billy snarled at him.

Tim shook his head as he exchanged a glance with John. "What do we do now?"

John answered, "We need to set up the only tent Billy and I got out of the van before it blew up; we all voted while you were still out cold to try to get to the creek."

"I'll vote the same," Tim paused. "We'll need the water, how much food do we have?"

"Not much, one cooler and some cans," Al answered.

"Can you make it, Tim?" John asked.

"My head hurts like hell." Tim rubbed the back of his head. "But, I'll make it, let's go." He looked up at the storm. "Anybody got a compass?"

"We only had one, and it's smashed to hell," Billy replied.

"We figured the creek's down that way." Al pointed in the direction of a barely perceptible down slope.

The four of them consolidated most of the material rescued from the van into the four backpacks. Each carrying an equal load, they trudged in close formation towards the unseen creek.

"Where's all the other hunters?" Al asked. "I know there ain't many out this far, but there's always one or two."

"Even in this weather?" Tim asked.

"Yeah, I guess we're the only stupid ones out here now."

"The road went down to the creek from where we wrecked, it never went up, only down," John spoke to himself as his eyes focused on no particular object or person. "We were going to curve around to our right, then go down; let's try to follow that course, and look for a tree line."

"Yeah." Al's expression brightened. "If we can at least get into the woods, that would provide us with some protection from this goddamned wind."

70

They slowly plodded for another five hundred yards, trying to maintain what John, the leader, felt was a constant direction down towards the creek.

"Look," Billy shouted, pointing to a dark line through the thick white snow-fog, "Trees."

The other three men stopped, then turned in silence towards the dark tree line and walked in that direction.

As they entered the forest, the snow slacked considerably, at least under the trees. Large pines spread their branches from the edge of the forest to about fifty yards in, they blocked much of the snow, leaving the ground still brown in patches.

"Over there's a good spot." Al pointed to a small clearing between the line of pine trees and a large stand of hardwoods.

The sun had set, a dark cold twilight left enough light filtered through the storm clouds for them to make out shapes and shades of white and black. The ground ahead had several snowless patches which looked like large irregular black spots.

"Do we have a flashlight?" John asked. "Mine blew up with the van."

"Mine's in the van along with Tim's," Al spoke up. "What 'bout you, Billy?"

"I forgot to bring one, all right," Billy snapped.

"That's okay." John calmly dropped his bundles on one of the clear spaces. "I saved Al's tent so you can put it up."

He started to comb the ground for rocks and sticks, throwing them as far as he could when he found one.

"No problem," Billy replied.

Billy dropped his load, and began pulling the long rolled up nylon tent out of its sack, then laying it on the bare patch of level ground John had cleared.

"I'm glad you saved this one, it'll sleep all of us," Al commented.

"I know," John replied. "Let's get some sleep tonight and see what we have and where we are in the morning," he added.

71

"God, yes," Al quickly answered.

All four men quietly worked together, setting up the large ten by twelve foot tent. They pulled all their gear inside, except the cooler, then they all crawled into the cabin tent.

No light was left in the sky, but the snow flakes appeared to generate their own luminescence. Inside the tent the only sound, besides their breathing, was the wind pushing the sides of the tent in many directions.

"God, why didn't you look where you were going?" Billy expelled the sentence with a huge sigh.

"Shut up, Billy," Al answered sharply.

"I can speak for myself," Tim quietly spoke. "I was looking where I was going, the tires started to skid, and I couldn't do a damn thing 'bout it."

"Look," Al interjected. "This shit ain't going to get any of us nowhere so let's concentrate on getting out of here in one piece, okay?"

"Yeah, okay," Billy said.

"What time you reckon it is?" Billy asked.

"No reckon about it," Al answered. "My watch still works and it's eight o'clock."

"Is it me, or does anyone else have freezing toes?" Tim asked in the darkness.

"Yeah," Billy quickly answered. "My feet are freezin' too."

"Pack your feet in your jackets," Al chimed in. "Your feet and hands lose heat faster than anything else, other than your head, so keep them warm."

"Are you sure?" Tim asked.

"Trust me," Al assured them. "First thing I did was wrap my feet in my jacket and I'm toasty now."

"Toasty?" Tim teased.

"Well, I could be warmer," Al chuckled. "But, I feel warmer than you two."

"I suppose," Tim answered.

"Do you guys notice how quiet it is?" John asked.

72

"So?" Tim answered.

"Where're all the night sounds?" John paused. "I mean, we've been here before when it snowed, you remember seven years ago?"

"That was a little snow, and it didn't last but a day on the ground, it weren't nothin' like this," Tim answered.

"Besides," Billy said, "We had a big fire goin' that whole huntin' trip."

"Yeah, but even then there were night sounds, owls, night animals, even deer," John paused again. "I don't hear anything."

"Ain't nothin' stupid enough to be out on a night like this," Billy broke in.

"Stupidity has nothing to do with eating," John said. "All I was noticing was I can hear no animal noises at all out there."

"Good," Al said. "Maybe we can all get some sleep tonight."

"All right," John reluctantly agreed, "I'll shut up."

"It ain't you, John," Al said. "This storm is weird as hell."

"That might be why all the animals are quiet," Tim added.

"Yeah," Billy snorted. "They're too busy stuffin' their feet into their jackets."

Chapter 8

O, call back yesterday, bid time return.
William Shakespeare Richard II, act 3, sc. 2.

Inside the tent the gentle glow of an unfamiliar dawn woke them; one by one they turned over, away from the dim light.

"Are you up?" Tim whispered to Al.

"Yeah, but I don't want to be." Al rolled his tongue around in his mouth. "I ain't got no toothbrush."

"I'm up, and I'll bet Billy is too." John began to get off the hard ground.

"Let's see where we are, and then look for the road," Al said.

"Then let's move our camp to the creek, at the end of the road where people can find us." John began to rub his face with both hands. "There's always one or two hunters who use that road."

"I'm for that." Tim sat up and stretched his arms; his mouth opened wide, distorting his whole face in a yawn. "Did we save any coffee?"

"All I was able to save was a half full container of powdered orange juice." John pulled a plastic sack beside him and lifted a jar of the breakfast drink out of it.

"But no water," Billy observed.

"Melt snow." John unzipped the front flap of the tent, looking outside.

"Melt snow," Billy mocked.

"What the hell!" John shouted then froze in his squatting position for a second.

"What?" Al's voice sounded annoyed.

"Look for yourself," John called back from outside the tent.

The other men climbed out of the tent, one by one, and stared at the scene in the cool morning light.

No clouds were in the early morning sky, nor was any snow on the ground. The temperature was in the lower forties and almost no wind was blowing. The four men looked in all directions without any comments for several long moments.

"Where the fuck are we?" Billy demanded, his face screwed up with a forced squint, not looking at any of his friends.

"Beats the hell outta me," Tim answered.

"Where's the clear cut area? Where's the road? Where's the van?" Al asked in amazement. "I'm confused, where the hell are we? Where the hell's anything?"

Their tent stood in a small clearing, next to several old, fallen oak trees. A thick forest of tall pine trees, mixed with hardwoods, surrounded them as far as they could see in all directions. The smell was new, fresher than it had been the year before, which gave the whole scene a more unreal feel.

"Where the hell's Tim's van?" Billy's eyes darted from corner to corner of their small patch of forest.

"That's a damned good question." Tim started to walk in the direction he thought his van lay.

"Don't go wanderin' into the woods." Al grabbed Tim's shoulder. "We don't want to get more lost, ya know."

"I ain't goin' too far." Tim shrugged off Al's hand. "I want to see how bad the wreck is."

"Best as I remember, it was totaled," Billy informed him. "Ain't nothin' left but a burned out shell."

75

"But, I want to see it," Tim insisted. "Besides, we can walk the road back out of here."

"That kind of makes sense," Al agreed. "But how do we keep from losing track of where our camp is, in case you don't find your van?"

"I'll stay here," John spoke up. "You guys go on and look for the van."

"Ok." Billy looked out into the woods. "We didn't walk more than ten minutes and that was in a snow storm, so the van has to be right out there in plain sight."

"We went downhill the whole way," Al added. "So, if we head straight uphill we should see it real soon."

. . . .

"Where's my van?" Tim scanned a full one hundred eighty degrees in front of him. "Where's the clear cut area?"

"What the hell's goin' on here?" Billy looked at Tim, then at Al. "This don't look like nothin' we saw yesterday, what the hell's goin' on here?"

"That's a good question." Al looked into the forest.

As the three men walked up the slight hill, away from what they assumed was close to Harris Creek, the forest became more thick with trees and tall dry grasses; it was as if no one had cut a tree in this place, ever. The strong scent of pine mixed with freshly fallen leaves as loud crunching sounds of squirrels searching for fallen nuts accented the crow calls; this was plainly not the place they had driven into the previous day.

"We need to get back to camp and get a plan together." Billy turned to look at his two companions.

"Right." Tim strained to see anything familiar.

"Let's head back down towards the creek," Al sighed. "At least if we locate that, we can figure out where we're at."

. . . .

76

Billy, Tim and Al hiked back to the tent, their footfalls could be heard before John could actually see them. As they walked towards John, all three of them were engaged in loud conversation about what they had seen, or had not seen.

"Listen." John raised his finger to his lips, to quiet the others.

"To what?" Tim asked in a whisper.

"To the sounds, there weren't any last night, but listen to the birds waking up, do you hear the hawk? Listen to the crows calling each other." John slowly raised his eyebrows. "And, do you hear the water running?"

"The creek," Tim answered loudly and clapped his hands together.

"At least we know where the hell we are." Al cleared his throat.

"Why do you say that?" John asked.

"There ain't no clearing up there," Tim answered. "My van ain't nowhere up there either."

"What did you see?" John asked.

"The woods," Al sighed. "This stand of pines give way to hardwoods, then a real thick stand of pines."

"So damned thick you can't see nothin' more than ten feet away," Billy interrupted.

"No van, and no more gear?" John asked.

"Not a bit," Al replied.

"And, I ain't getting' lost up there lookin' for it, neither." Billy looked towards the sound of running water. "Let's get some water."

"Wait," John said. "Don't go anywhere alone; better yet, don't go anywhere without a gun."

"I'm not interested in shootin' nothin' you idiot," Billy sounded frustrated.

"Something might be interested in you, though; we don't know where or when we are, you know?"

"Don't start your stupid mind games with me right now, I agree with Al, I'm confused as hell, and I don't like none of your

77

shit when I feel like this." Billy walked towards the sound of running water.

"I'll go with him," Al said. "I've got my forty four magnum."

Al lifted his coat and revealed a large pistol in a hip holster.

"While they're getting lost." Tim turned to John. "Let's go through everythin' we got."

Tim leaned into the tent and pulled out a backpack. Reaching back in, Tim pulled out two plastic bags and sorted through them.

"Ain't much here but drinks, and a few cans of pork and beans." Tim dropped the sack on the ground.

"I know," John responded. "The cooler's only got some deer meat, hamburger and some bacon. All the eggs and milk are long gone, unless you want to have day old eggnog without the nog."

"We all got our rifles and ammo, and enough dry clothes, though," Tim said.

"But no compass, nor any idea of where we are," John added.

"Don't be so damned cheerful." Tim laughed without smiling.

John turned his head sharply when he heard the loud sound of leaves crunching beneath the feet of men walking in his direction; Al and Billy walked quickly towards the tent.

"Come down here, you have to see this," Billy shouted.

John waved his hand at them, motioning for them to wait as he reached into the tent, pulling out his rifle case and a clip of cartridges.

"You expecting trouble?" Tim asked.

"If you're asking me if the hairs on the back of my neck are standing at attention, they are." John pulled his rifle out of the soft case.

John slid one cartridge out of the clip, he then put the partial clip into the magazine, not letting a shell into the chamber as he closed the bolt and set the safety on.

John motioned with a turn of his head for Tim to follow, then the two of them walked to meet their friends. John pulled his rifle by its leather strap over his shoulder and walked beside Tim on the way to the creek and the other men.

The leaves from the hardwoods lay fresh on the forest floor along with heavily scented brown pine straw, the thickness of which cushioned their steps, but still plainly announced their presence.

Rapidly turning from a gentle incline to a steep embankment, the ground gave way to a wide and shallow creek, flowing rapidly and clear. The sound it made was almost that of a river; the creek itself was loud and deep only in a narrow center channel of the bed.

"Look at that," Billy demanded. "I never remember that much water in our creek."

"If it's got that much water, that's okay with me." John teased Billy who became flushed red in the face.

"Don't start your shit with me, not now, where the hell are we?" Billy gritted his teeth hard enough to show the churning muscles around his jaws.

"We're all right here, looking at the moving water," Al said. "We can't have walked that far in the storm last night, and when we crashed we were almost to Harris Creek. We were almost to the creek we've hunted at for over ten years, and which I've hunted at for 'bout thirty, so, all we have to do is walk the creek and look for the forest road, after all, it does cross this creek somewhere before the creek dumps into the river."

"I still want to know what happened to all the snow?" John asked, staring at the creek.

"It melted, that ain't so hard to guess," Billy answered.

"I don't see how that much snow could be gone by morning," John sounded skeptical. "That was a blizzard last night, even if it stopped snowing right after we all went into the

79

tent, there had to be six inches of snow on the ground, how can that much snow disappear in six hours?"

"This here's the South, boy, snow ain't supposed to happen." Billy chuckled, looked down at the ground for a brief moment, then looked back up at John.

"Shit ain't supposed to happen either, but it does." John looked blankly at him. "Besides, if it all melted last night, the ground should be muddy as hell this morning, and it isn't."

Billy shook his head as he stared at the deepening blue sky.

"The ground's a little wet, it don't have to be a mud pit, ya know; anyway, let's look for the road," Billy said.

"First let's move the tent and all our stuff down closer to the water, 'least ways we'll be able to find it better when we're walkin' the creek," Al said.

"Great idea," John agreed.

Billy shrugged his shoulders as he followed the others back to the tent.

It took four trips to carry everything from their first campsite to the new location on a clear spot overlooking the broad creek. Al packed a compact set of back packing pots and dishes inside his duffel bag so they would have a pot to boil water in, make orange drinks, and they also would have a pot to cook all the bacon for breakfast.

....

"Are you ready to go?" Billy looked at Tim, sipping his last cup of orange drink.

"No, but let's look for the road anyway."

"Why don't we all walk down stream?" Billy asked. "The road's that-a-way anyway."

"We don't know that for sure," John interrupted. "Since we don't know exactly where we are, we need to cover any possibility."

"Guess you're right," Billy reluctantly agreed.

80

"Everybody," Al spoke up. "Remember your orange vests, some idiot may think you're a ten point buck."

All four men rummaged through their clothes, pulled out the required orange hunting vests and slipped them on.

"Al and I both have watches," John said. "So, you go with Al, and Tim will go with me."

"Okay," Al added. "I'll go up stream, and you guys go the other way, let's meet back here at three o'clock."

"What time do you have?" John asked.

"Twenty five after nine."

"Me too," John responded. "Let's go."

The two pairs of men separated and walked slowly along the edge of the creek in opposite directions.

Chapter 9

And this our life, exempt from public haunt,
Finds tongues in trees, books in the running brooks,
Sermons in stones, and good in everything.
William Shakespeare, As You Like It, act 2, sc.1.

Through the thick canopy of branches and boughs, a strong pale yellow light shone in patchwork spots on the forest floor; for late Fall, the sun was intense. The light glistened on the churning water next to John and Tim who stopped to sip handfuls of the cool liquid.

"This stuff tastes better than last year," Tim said between slurps.

"Tastes like it's got a different mineral content, and it's a lot cleaner." John stood and picked his rifle back up from the tree on which it was propped. "It all feels different but the thing that bothers me is what we haven't found."

"Kind of like lookin' for the van," Tim paused. "We ain't found no signs of nothin', let alone a road."

"Also, we haven't seen any beer cans, food cans, or junk food wrappers."

"Maybe we're the first to get lost this deep in the forest."

John paused, scratching his chin. "But where exactly is this? The National Forest isn't that big around here, so somebody most likely should have been through here before."

"I don't know." Tim shrugged his shoulders. "We might have got lost back on the forest road before my van blew up."

"Then how do you explain the van not being there, or the clear cut area not being there?"

"I can't explain it."

"Let's keep going for a while and then get back." John motioned for them to keep walking

The men walked in silence as they observed a wide variety of small animals, listening to the constant loud rustling of leaves around them. As if nothing threatened them, birds, rodents, and small mammals scurried above and beneath the blanket of brown and reddish leaves over the forest bed.

John was the first to spot a beaver, which acted as if John and Tim did not exist. Squirrels scolded the two men when they began to move again and walk beneath large nests, hanging from low and high branches in oaks and pines. Stopping to rest at the end of thirty minutes of walking, John slowly pointed to his left.

Tim looked in the pointed direction and saw a large white tailed buck; the large animal snorted loudly, spun quickly and darted up a steep hill and into the surrounding forest, flashing a white patch under its tail at them. Tim lifted his rifle to his shoulder and peeped through the scope at the fleeing animal.

"God, that's a big one; too bad we're so far from camp, or we'd have plenty of meat." Tim's forehead rolled back slightly.

"Let's get back, I want to know if the others found the road," John interrupted, looking preoccupied.

"Me too, we sure as hell ain't found nothin'." Tim lowered his rifle with a sigh and hung it over his shoulder on its wide leather sling.

The men stood by the creek for a few moments, scanning the countryside before walking back to the tent. They each looked into their own forest, aware of the other person, yet looking for their personal reflection in the transparent scene.

"There's a hell of a lot more game in these woods than there was last year." John broke the silence.

"What makes you say that?"

"For one thing, look up." John pointed to a flock of large birds, flying in seven large V formations which covered almost one half of the blue sky.

"So, I've seen flocks of birds flying South before."

"Those are geese, and there isn't supposed to be that many flying South, or anywhere, any more." John looked back down at Tim. "Let alone that many flying in formation across this state."

"Yeah," Tim paused, still looking up. "What does it mean?"

Ignoring the direct question, John answered, "Take in a deep breath, the whole place smells different and haven't you also noticed an extra amount of bird calls? Also, aren't there more deer, and haven't you seen any of the bear tracks?"

"Bear?" Tim asked in a loud voice. "Shit, there ain't supposed to be none of them down here, they's all up in the mountains."

"Let's get going back and I'll show you the tracks," John paused and cocked his head. "I'm not one hundred percent sure they're bear tracks, I'm not sure. Something's strange here, I'll feel better when we're all back together."

"Me too, let's get."

John drew in a long breath and sighed, "You know, as nervous as I know I should be, I feel at peace in these woods."

Tim and John walked rapidly along the fresh path of trampled down dry brown grasses the two men had made walking down stream.

………………………….

Two and one half miles up river from John and Tim, the other men found themselves in the same strange forest.

"Billy, will you stop makin' so much noise trompin' through the brush," Al chided.

"Why not, ain't we supposed to be found?" Billy asked.

"Found, but not shot at," Al replied.

84

"Hell, I'll shoot back."

"Walk a little slower, and a little quieter."

Billy slowed down, waiting for Al to catch up with him.

"I'm thirsty." Billy stepped onto the incline leading down to the creek. The soft dirt gave way under his boot; Billy had to run down the short hill to the creek in order to keep from falling. He stopped short of the water waving his left arm in the air, regaining his balance.

"I'll take an easier way." Al walked twenty yards down stream and onto the bank along a much slighter incline.

"Very funny," Billy complained.

"Come over here," Al called to Billy, squatting down, looking at the dirt.

"What is it?" Billy slowly walked to his friend, along the edge of the creek.

Al pointed to the area under his feet, "Look at all the tracks, this is a crossing used by every animal whose tracks I know, and then some."

"I see a lot of deer, 'coons, possum, and that one looks like one big assed dog." Billy squatted next to his friend, staring and pointing to the tacks as he recognized them.

"Sure looks like a dog, but it's one hell of a big one; look how wide it is, and look how far down into the mud the impression is. It's damn near as big as my foot, and half again as wide, might be a bear." Al stood up, stretched, and made a deep grunting noise. "I'm too old for this sort of stuff."

Billy nodded, leaned his rifle against a nearby tree and began to drink handfuls of water with a loud noise. Al walked a few feet back up the incline, and sat down in front of a large oak tree, leaning into a hollow between two large roots. He gently lay his rifle on top of one of the roots which jutted above the ground.

Al spotted a large formation of geese in the sky. He called to Billy as he pointed out the large number of geese in the sky. Al saw Billy, still drinking water from the creek with his hands

85

and also caught a glimpse of a large moving object across the creek, half way up the incline on the other side.

The woods on the other side of the creek had more pine trees and low shrubs which still held many of their leaves. The moving shape across the creek was less than fifty yards away, but Al could not make out its form; it was big and furry. As a head poked around a tree trunk, a huge form rose on two massive rear legs. Al called to Billy who finished drinking and now looked directly at Al's face.

"Don't move, Billy, and don't panic, stay where you are." Al slowly lifted his coat and gradually pulled out his long barreled forty four magnum revolver.

"What the hell's going on." Billy set his feet a bit further apart and leaned his head slightly forward.

"I told you not to panic," Al said a little louder and firmer. "There's a bear behind you."

"Don't hand me that shit," Billy smugly chuckled then turned around.

Billy stared into the large upright animal's face, no more than twenty five feet away, for ten full seconds; he didn't move, neither did the bear.

Al leveled his revolver at the bear and pulled back the hammer; the click made by the revolver caused the bear to cock his head to one side. It fell to all four feet, and let out a noise which sounded like a long, loud sigh.

"God damnit, shoot the bastard, where'd he go?" Billy shouted, still standing by the edge of the creek.

Billy tensed his whole body and dropped both arms to his sides. His jaw became slack, and his face gave the impression of a person gasping for air.

Loud sounds of trampled leaves and small branches echoed through the creek flat as a huge brownish black mass of fur thundered back up the incline and deep into the woods.

Al slowly let the hammer back down on his revolver as he took in a deep breath of fresh air.

"You look like you crapped in your pants," Al observed. He repositioned the empty cylinder under the hammer, then stuffed the revolver back into its holster.

"I damn near did." Billy jumped to the tree his rifle was leaning against, grabbed it, and jumped next to Al in only four quick moves. "There ain't no bears in these woods."

"Looks like there's at least one bear in these woods." Al stood, picking up his rifle. "What you say we get back to the tent because I don't see no trail, no road, and no people."

Billy let out a short burst of air from his still tight lungs as his right leg, from the knee down, developed a strong tremor. He leaned on a tree near Al, attempting to catch his breath.

Al looked as hard as he could into the woods on both sides of the creek before turning back and walking towards Billy.

"I've been in these woods longer than any of you, I showed the rest of you this corner of the National Forest," Al paused, looking at Billy. "But now, I don't know where the hell we are."

"What's that supposed to mean?" Billy asked, still breathing heavily.

"Don't know," Al paused, catching up to Billy. "I guess it means we're lost."

"I'm gonna get me some pot meat on the way back," Billy declared, his mood turning to anger.

"What're you talking about?"

"There's a pile of them furry little rodents in the trees, and I'm gonna shoot a few to take back to camp and eat'm."

"Oh," Al paused. "You got your twenty two?"

"You bet."

Billy stopped by a tree and pulled a twenty two caliber semi automatic pistol from underneath his coat. He aimed carefully by steadying his hand against a tree trunk, and shot two rounds. Missing the scurrying animal with both shots, he kept shooting until no more shells were in the pistol. Billy released the empty clip, pulled another one from his coat pocket, and jammed it into the pistol.

87

"Keep still for a minute," Al quietly demanded.

"What for?" Billy replied in an annoyed voice, not looking at Al.

"I hear somethin'."

"What?" Billy demanded.

"That squirrel's laughin' his ass off." Al looked deep into the forest to hide the growing smile on his face.

"Funny." Billy took careful aim at the same squirrel which had jumped to the next tree.

A single shot cracked from the small pistol, sending the squirrel abruptly to the ground. Without saying a word, Billy walked to where the animal lay, picked it up and stuffed it into a camouflaged colored bag he yanked from his pocket.

Chapter 10

Take care to sell your horse before he dies. The art of life is passing losses on.
Robert Frost, "The Ingenuities of Debt".

John and Tim were the first to return to the tent as the sun was hanging low in the west. The light cast a deeper shade of yellow with some orange and reds on the surrounding forest, the shadows of the trees were longer as the warmth of the day dissipated rapidly.

"What time you got?" Tim asked

John checked his watch. "It's four ten."

"I'll get a fire goin'."

John rummaged in one of the back packs and pulled out an aluminum pot. He walked to the creek and filled it with water while Tim began walking in loose circles, picking up small sticks and placing them in a pile about twenty yards from the tent.

John returned to the campsite with the water, set it down next to the tent, then began to help Tim gather wood. John dropped his load of medium sized sticks next to the pile of smaller sticks, falling to the ground with a loud clatter. He began to kick leaves away from the site of that night's fire; John circled the spot, making the cleared dirt area wider each time.

Tim walked deeper into the forest, gathering larger and larger pieces of wood, bringing them back to a spot beside the tent. He carefully built a pyramid shaped pile of wood for the night's fire.

John picked up two handfuls of the driest leaves he could find and, lifting the pile of small sticks, stuffed the leaves under the sticks; he gathered several more handfuls of leaves and also stuck them under the pile of sticks. After arranging the small sticks around the mound of leaves, John pulled a small box of matches from his front right pocket and lit the leaves.

"That was the last match in this box," John added the empty match box to the growing flames. "Do you have any?"

"No, but we can always start a fire somehow," Tim hopefully answered. "Al's good at that."

The leaves flamed quickly, catching most of the smaller sticks on fire almost immediately. John began leaning the larger sticks against the small glowing twigs in a circular pattern, as if building a wigwam. John continued this pattern, using ever larger pieces of wood, until the fire was high enough to provide warmth for the lost men.

"Wonder when they'll get back?" Tim asked, squatting in front of the fire.

"Any time now, it'll be dark in less than an hour."

"What do ya want to eat? We ain't got much."

"A can of soup or beans will be fine," John replied.

A loud crunching of leaves and sticks coming from upstream caught the attention of both men.

Looking towards the noise, Tim's face showed recognition, "It's them."

"I can see," John acknowledged as he looked up.

Al and Billy walked quickly to the tent, dumping their rifles and gear. They both then turned to the fire to join the other two men.

"Did you see anything?" Tim asked.

"Hell yeah," Billy said.

"The road?" John asked quickly.

"Hell no," Billy insisted.

Al laughed out loud as he looked at Tim, "Billy met up face to face with the largest bear I've ever seen outside of a zoo."

"Damn straight, I ain't never seen no bear that big." Billy eagerly spread out his arms to gauge the size of the beast.

"Bear?" Tim sounded the word out slowly.

90

"I thought those were the tracks I saw, remember, I showed them to you on the way back, and you didn't believe me," John spoke to Tim.

"You saw the thing?" Tim asked Billy.

"Close enough to touch it," Billy affirmed, nodding his head.

"You weren't that close to it," Al chided, shaking his head.

"Felt like I was," Billy replied indignantly. "I could smell his nasty ol' breath."

"But, no road?" John asked again.

"We didn't see no signs of nothin'," Al quietly spoke, losing his faint smile.

"Neither did we," John sighed.

"Let's get somethin' to eat, then we'll worry about all of this," Tim said

"That's a good idea," Billy said. "Let me clean and skin these squirrel up, then we can have a good hot dinner."

"You actually hit that small a target up in a tree?" Tim teased. "We heard the twenty two shots, but we figured you missed."

"Shut up, or you'll get nothin'." Billy walked towards the creek with the game bag full of that night's food.

"Come on," Tim said. "Let's make up some sort of a contraption to barbecue the damn things over the fire, I'm hungry."

John and Tim looked at each other, walked into the woods behind the tent to look on the ground for long sticks. Finding several long, and several Y shaped sticks, the two men returned to the fire and pieced together a crude rack on which they could cook the meat.

As the reddening sun lowered over the small rise to their west, the forest lining the creek was in total shadows; darkness overtook the tent and the three men now huddling next to the fire.

91

"Here comes Billy with the food." Al pointed towards the man walking from the creek with five cleaned, skinned and headless small animals.

"Hurry up, I'm hungry," Al spoke in a loud voice.

"Good, you cook'em." Billy handed him the carcasses.

As Al shoved a dressed squirrel onto the long stick, John spoke. "We don't know where we are, and we've got to figure that little problem out before anything else."

"So?" Tim asked. "Does anyone have any ideas as to where we are?"

"Lost," Billy said flatly.

"Good," Al added sarcastically. "But, where? I told you that this don't look like anywhere I've ever been in these woods."

"Can we assume this creek's the one we usually hunt along?" John asked. "Or, is this the river?"

"Unless the forest service moved everything around in that snowstorm, that was the last thing we saw before the wreck," Tim said. "The river's a long way from where we was, besides the river ain't that small."

"Yeah, you were lookin' at the creek instead of the road," Billy complained.

"I say we should drop anymore talk about the wreck," John firmly said. "That's behind us, we need to concentrate on finding out where we are."

"I say we go back up the hill 'n look for the van 'n the road we came in on," Billy insisted.

"You guys did that this morning," John answered him. "What did you find?"

"Nothin'," Al answered.

"Listen up you guys," Billy sounded insistent. "That clear cut area has to be up there somewhere."

"You think we're lost now?" John looked straight at Billy. "Think how lost we'll be if we head into a strange patch of woods with no point of reference, no waypoints, no compass or no idea where we're going?"

92

"We could mark our way out, 'n follow it back here," Billy insisted.

"Mark your way with what?" John asked. "Who has a bag of red flags, or who's going to give up their extra clothes?"

"We could notch tree trunks," Billy sounded angry.

"That's the best way to get lost I can think of," John sarcastically replied.

"Look." Al turned the stick with the roasting meat on it. "If this is the right creek, all we have to do is head down stream; the damn creek flows into the river, the same river that goes through the closest town, and the town's only twenty miles away from here at best. There's tons of houses along the river, especially goin' west from the bridge so we're bound to run into people if we head down stream towards the river."

"Me and John walked that way today and we didn't see nothin'," Tim said.

"We'll have to go further," Al insisted.

After a long silence, nothing but the crackling of the fire and the hissing of meat as it cooked was heard.

"I think he's right," John said. "Nobody's going to look for us out here for at least a week, so we need to find ourselves, not wait to be found."

"I agree," Tim added.

"I guess it's okay," Billy said slowly. "But I don't buy all this."

"What don't you buy?" John looked across the campfire at Billy.

"Where we are," Billy said flatly. "How the hell can we be by Harris Creek where we've hunted for so long?"

"Why not?" Tim asked.

"It don't look the same," Billy forcefully said. "The Forest Service can't change that much in a year, it's impossible."

"They did clear cut a lot of it," Tim observed.

"Clear cut, yeah." Billy turned to face Tim. "But, we're talking about a whole new forest with lots more trees, and where's the clear cut? Where's the road leading back out of here and where's your fuckin' van?"

"I have to admit, I'm confused about it all too." Tim shook his head slowly. "But, what the hell do we do?"

"I have to agree with Al," John spoke up. "We walk down the creek until we get to the river, then we walk north until we get to a house or something."

"We need to get to the river and get to a phone," Al said.

"Yeah," Tim agreed. "I have to call my wife."

"To tell her you blew up the van?" Billy teased.

"I thought we weren't going to bring that up," John scolded Billy.

"It was too easy," Billy chuckled.

"I think the first three are done," Al interrupted, looking at the cooking meat, sizzling over the fire. "Someone stick a knife in and check."

Billy pulled a lock blade knife from his pocket and stuck it into the squirrel to the left side of the stick. He twisted it both ways, looking closely at the cooking animal.

"It's ready. I'll cook the other two while we share these," Billy announced.

Billy cut strips of meat off the cooked squirrels, passing them out to everybody. He lay his pieces on his lap, stuck the remaining two carcasses onto the stick, then placed the loaded stick back over the fire.

The four men ate quickly as the sunlight disappeared and the night's darkness merged with the forest. The sounds changed from those of daylight animals, to those of the night. Although the sun had set, the birds had not all settled down to roost, many of them were still flying from tree to tree, calling. The sound of rushing water from the creek became louder as the animal noises subsided. The constant background of insect sounds rose in volume, and unseen small animals started trampling the forest floor, adding their noise to the night sounds.

"We've got a long hike tomorrow." Al stood up and tossed several small bones into the dark forest. "So, I'm gettin' on to bed 'n get as much sleep as I can get."

"Me too," John added.

"I'm goin' out there and take a dump first," Billy announced. "Who's got the toilet paper?"

"It's in my back pack," John answered. "Don't use too much, we've only got my two rolls."

"Wash up some before you come back into the tent." Tim looked towards the creek. "I for one don't want you stinkin' up the tent tonight."

"Very funny," Billy answered.

John and Al gathered up their things and disappeared into the tent while Tim sat silent by the fire, staring at the dying flames. Billy walked to the tent to collect the toilet paper from John, then he disappeared into the darkness.

Chapter 11

"When the sunlight disappears," John said, "the world becomes an unknown to daylight animals like us. Sounds and feelings become the chain on which the anchor of fear is welded, then thrown into the darkness with us attached to the other end."

"John, will you keep your crazy thoughts to yourself." Al pulled his sleeping bag up over the lower part of his face and stared blankly at the ceiling of the tent.

"I am," John answered. "And, they're not crazy."

Al sighed as he turned to face John who was staring out the front mesh flap of the tent.

"John, you're one of the more sensible members of this group, so don't go off the deep end," Al whispered.

"What are you talking about?"

"That bull shit you came up with a second ago."

"That wasn't bull shit." John sat up. "All I said was, that we're afraid of the dark because we can't see what's making all those sounds, you know, the stuff that goes bump out there."

"Why don't you say what you mean," Al said, annoyed. "You always make it so hard to know what you're saying."

John stared silently at Tim, sitting in front of the fire while Al lay on his back, resting his head in his palms. Tim slowly added small sized logs to the fire, keeping it at a moderate level.

"I can't figure out what happened to us, I mean we should be right where we were last year," Al said. "I saw the tree line of the creek in front of us, and we didn't walk that far in the snow storm so where the hell is the wrecked van, where are we now?"

"I think the answer is as much when are we, as where are we."

"Look, each year you go through the same damned thing," Al sounded frustrated.

"What's that?" John asked, still staring out the front flap of the tent.

"Thinking you're in some other time. Last year you were convinced that it was right after the last ice age. Remember the time you were in the middle of the Indian wars, then the War Between the States?"

"It's not that bad, besides, what's wrong with a good imagination?" John sounded somewhat amused that anyone had paid attention to his musings in previous years.

"Nothin', when everythin's going all right, but when we're lost and everythin', well, it ain't necessary."

"I guess not, but," John paused, turning to face Al. "Nothing."

"Shhh, listen." Al sat up quickly.

"What?" John asked.

"Did you hear somethin'?"

"I thought I heard a wolf, but there can't be any here, at least not now," John answered. "It must be a pack of wild dogs, there's been more and more of them out this way."

"Get serious, John, I think it was a wolf; I remember readin' about some of them comin' back down South, some've been spotted up in the mountains in the past few years."

"Maybe, but I wonder if it could be a stray dog. Like I said, there's been a lot of them around here lately."

"I guess." Al lay back down.

Billy came running out of the darkness, clutching the roll of toilet paper, a short streamer of it flailing in the wind behind him. He briefly paused next to Tim by the fire, then he rushed to the tent, grabbed the zipper and opened the flap quickly. Diving into the tent, he placed his left knee on John's leg and lost his balance, rolling over.

"Ouch, will you watch out!" John held his injured leg and winced.

"Yeah, yeah."

Billy reached into the back of the tent, found his rifle case and pulled the rifle out of it. Tilting his back pack on its side, he pulled five shinny brass cartridges out of the side pocket, yanked back the bolt on the rifle and began shoving the cartridges into the magazine.

"What the hell're you doing?" Al asked loudly.

"There's a bunch of damned wolves out there, one of the bastards was almost next to me while I was takin' a dump."

"That's no reason to kill all of us in here," John said firmly.

"I ain't gonna kill nobody, I don't wanna get killed in the middle of the night by no wolf 'r no bear."

Al calmly rested his right hand on the barrel of Billy's rifle and pushed it slowly down to the floor of the tent.

"It'd make me feel better if your rifle were empty while it's in here with us," Al spoke in a calm voice. "If it'll make you feel better I'll keep my forty four loaded and right next to me all night, in its holster."

"Please?" John pleaded with Billy.

Billy slowly lay his rifle in his lap, then even slower, he opened and closed the action until all the cartridges were on the ground. He scooped them up and replaced them into the side pocket of his pack, giving several short sighs, then relaxed slightly.

98

Tim, hearing all the noise in the tent, walked over and squatted in front of the flap, raising both eyebrows as he peered into the tent. "Billy's right, I heard the wolves too."

"We heard only one," Al paused, looking at John. "How many did you hear?"

Tim stood up, stretching. "I could make out about four, they was calling to each other."

"See, what'd I tell you," Billy insisted. "Wolves; god, I wish I had at least one plug to chew on."

"You lose all of your chewin' tobacco in the crash?" Al asked, not moving from his position in his sleeping bag.

"Yeah, all of it," Billy confirmed with a forced frown. "I thought I had at least some in my coat pocket, but all I had was the plug in my mouth."

"And you swallowed it, right?" John stifled a grin.

"Screw you." Billy's middle finger rose from his fist, unseen by John.

"Why don't you go clean up at the creek, we don't need your stink-butt in our tent tonight," John requested. "Besides, I don't think there's anything too dangerous that close to the camp fire.

" Funny." Billy stumbled off to the creek.

"Why don't you come on in here, Tim," John said. "We'll need all the rest we can get."

"The fire needs to go all night long; any wolves out there, it might scare'em off," Al commented.

"That was my thinkin'." Tim squatted back down in front of the tent flap. "But, I'm tired and I don't wanna stay out here no more."

"All right, I'll keep the fire goin' for a while," Al replied before he crawled to the front of the tent, put his boots on, opened the flap and thrust himself into the cold night air.

Tim crawled into the tent as Al left; he took off his boots and tossed them into the back of the tent.

"Could you hand me my sleeping bag?" Tim asked.

99

Billy stumbled back into the tent and grabbed a green sleeping bag and tossed it to Tim who unrolled and lay it between John and Al's rumpled sleeping bags. Tim slid into his bag and lay on his back, taking in a deep breath, as if he were about to speak, but let it back out slowly.

"I wonder what happened to all the snow we had yesterday?" Tim asked.

"Like I said before, this here's the south," Billy laughed. "It don't snow and stay like it does up North in Yankee land."

"Yeah, but there must'a been at least six inches of snow on the ground, not even countin' how deep the drifts were," Tim skeptically replied.

"Weren't near that much," Billy insisted. "There was, least ways, 'nough snow for you to get us all stuck out here in the middle of nowhere."

"I told you already, it was not his fault," John quickly answered. "The van went into a slide, and even you couldn't have done any better."

A second of silence fell, then Tim spoke, "Look you guys, I'm real sorry about wreckin' the van, and gettin' all us stuck out here."

"It was your van, Tim, you're the one who's lost more than any of us; we're all right, but you're still out your van," John said.

"I ain't gonna say nothin' else on the subject, but y'all know what I think," Billy said.

Billy pulled off his boots and spread out his sleeping bag along the back of the tent, next to all the gear then he tossed his jacket over his feet.

Al sat by the fire, adding the rest of the small and large branches left from that afternoon's gathering; the fire was now higher than when Tim had been tending it. The light from the flames was decidedly visible from within the tent as an orange glow through the green tent fabric which gave an odd tint to everyone inside the tent.

"Are we all in agreement about tomorrow?" Tim asked.

100

"If you mean should we walk down stream and look for civilization, yes," John said.

"I still think we ought to look for the burned out van, that way we'll know where the road is, and then we can get back down to where the other hunters are." Billy cleared his throat.

"You're still awake too?" Tim lifted his head enough to look back at Billy.

"Yeah, I don't feel like everything's okay." Billy looked at the ceiling of the tent.

Several seconds passed in silence, each of the three looking at the other in the orange-green light from the camp fire.

"I still think walking down stream will be safer; for sure it's a shorter walk to the river, but we could get lost even more if we take off in the forest because nothing looks like it did in the snow storm." John sat up and looked out the front flap at Al by the fire. "If we follow the creek, we'll get to where the road crosses it, then we'll be closer to civilization than if we looked for the van and walked out that way."

"I guess so." Billy fell silent again.

"I got a funny feelin' about all this, nothing makes sense." Tim looked at John.

Al walked to the front of the tent, stooped down and unzipped the flap, slowly crawling in and throwing his boots over Billy, to the back corner of the tent.

"All the wood's gone, and I'm tired." Al slipped into his sleeping bag.

"We were talkin' about tomorrow," Tim said.

"Yeah, I could hear y'all; do we all agree about followin' the creek tomorrow?" Al asked.

"I do," John answered.

"Me too," Tim added.

"I'm still not sure about where we are," Billy added.

"None of us are, this place ain't exactly the woods I'm used to," Al calmly said. "But, we need to do something constructive."

"I still think I'm right," John declared.

101

"I told you to keep it to your self," Al scolded, crinkling the corner of his right eye.

"I don't care, there's got to be something to it."

"What are you two talking about?" Billy asked, reluctantly rising from his sleeping bag.

"It's nothing, John's crazy idea, it's the same one he has every year," Al sighed.

"Not that time shit again," Billy laughed.

"Laugh if you want, but how do you explain all the animals which aren't supposed to be here." John paused.

"I don't know, but this is real, and what you're sayin' ain't." Tim rolled over in his sleeping bag. "Please let me go to sleep so I don't fall asleep on my feet tomorrow."

"He's right, I'm tired too," Al said.

"Yeah," Billy added. "Say your prayers, and get to sleep."

"I don't think that'll do much good now," John said softly.

"I don't give a damn what you think, I'm going to sleep," Billy snorted.

"Good night, then," John answered.

John remained sitting up, looking out the tent flap while the others fell asleep. After a few minutes, he lay back down with his face under the opening in front so he could see the sky through the leafless branches of the oak trees above the tent. The moon was a thick crescent, which was being covered with layer upon layer of dark, rapidly moving clouds. John finally fell asleep to the sound of a rising wind blowing dry leaves across the ground.

102

Chapter 12

A journey is like marriage. The certain way to be wrong is to think you control it.
John Steinbeck, Travels With Charley: in Search of America, pt. 1

John was the first to wake the next morning, stirred by the thumping sound of a steady rain upon the slanted tent roof. Rubbing his eyes, he looked towards the front flap, noticing that someone had tied it shut sometime during the night. The humidity was so high and the temperature so low that the air felt like an almost frozen liquid. He could see his breath rise from his face as a fog blowing from between his teeth. He pulled his sleeping bag tighter around his neck and closed his eyes.

"Are you awake?" Tim whispered from the cocoon of his blue sleeping bag.

"Yes, I am." John opened his eyes as wide as he could and yawned.

"Me too," Al's voice rose from the darkness of the tent. "That rain woke me up when it started last night, and then again about ten minutes ago."

"Did you close the front flap?" John asked.

"Yeah."

The dim light filtered through the green fabric; it was still not enough to make the four men fully visible inside the tent. They lay silent until the light became strong enough to make out details within the tent.

The morning was cold, about thirty five degrees; it was gray and wet with a steady fall of small water droplets, larger than mist, cascading in an almost solid fog-like sheet.

"Oh shit." Billy awoke to the cold rain, scratching his lower back. "It's rainin'."

"Billy's up now." John sat up. Tim grunted agreement, remaining curled up inside his sleeping bag.

"Well." Billy rubbed his eyes. "I ain't goin' nowhere 'til it stops rainin'."

"You want to stay in here for a day or so?" John brushed his fingers through rumpled hair.

"It'll stop in an hour or so," Billy speculated.

"Don't think so, not the way our luck's been running so far," John replied.

"Could you shut that back flap, I'm cold." Tim looked to the back of the tent, staring at Billy who was still laying in his sleeping bag.

Returning Tim's stare for a moment, Billy then looked at the small window in the back center of the tent. Saying nothing, he sat up, unfastened the flap, and tied it down.

"I'm hungry, what've we got?" he demanded.

"All I could get out of the wreck before the fire was one bag of food," John answered.

"Well, what's in it?"

"Some bread, and cans of pork and beans, and vegetables," John said. "And one can of juice."

"What 'bout the meat in the cooler?" Billy asked.

"We ate all the bacon yesterday, all that's left is some deer meat from last year and some gross looking hamburger meat," John sounded disgusted. "I don't think it was much good to start with and now it isn't even worth cooking."

"Who wants to get up and cook the deer meat, then?" Al asked.

"Damn sure I ain't," Billy insisted.

"I don't think any of us wants to sit in the cold rain and cook meat on the stove," Tim said.

104

"What 'bout bringin' the stove in here, and cookin' the meat inside the tent?" Billy asked.

"What do we use for matches?" John asked. "I used my last one last night, besides, do you want to burn down our tent?"

"You got a point," Al said.

"I guess let's have the juice and bread." Billy reached for the paper sack near him in the rear of the tent.

"Don't eat everything we have in one meal," Al insisted.

"You worry too much," Billy said.

"And you don't worry enough," Al replied. He looked concerned. "What happens if we're out here for a week?"

"Oh, hell, while you three women fight about what's for breakfast, I gotta take a leak," Billy snorted.

He stuck his feet into his boots, crawled across the tent, pulled his jacket on, opened the front flap then quickly leapt out into the cold rain.

"How much bread is left?" Al asked, not looking at Billy as he left the tent.

John searched the brown paper bag with the name of the small grocery store near Al's house written on it in bright red letters.

"Four hamburger buns, that's all"

"We could each have one, and some of the juice," Tim added hopefully.

"We'll have to drink it all if we open it," John added. "It's in a can, and we don't have anything to store the rest of it in."

"Our luck's running pretty bad so far." Tim rolled his eyeballs back into their sockets.

"Well, we'll have to eat off the land for the most part," Al said. "That'll be all right, there's enough game here for that."

"Well, you are what you eat." John pulled the rolls and can of juice out of the sack and placed them in front of him. "I just remembered, does anyone have a can opener?"

105

Al laughed and reached into his front pocket, pulling out a Swiss army knife. "You always laugh at my knife, but now you won't."

John opened the pack of buns, took one then passed it to Tim while Al picked up the juice can and opened it, taking a long drink before handing it to John.

Billy rushed back in through the still open front flap.

"Watch where you're goin'," Al chastised. "You're drippin' all over us, not to mention steppin' all over us."

"Sorry, where's my food?"

"Right there." John pointed to the bun left in the plastic sack. "Hurry up and eat, I think we should be going soon."

"I say we stay here 'till the weather's okay," Billy said before he gulped down his hamburger bun.

"Why?" Al asked.

"'Cause I ain't gonna walk in that mess out there." Billy paused a second before he slurped most of the rest of the juice from the can.

"Well, you can stay here alone, but the rest of us are goin' to look for where the road crosses the creek, then walk out of here." Al looked out the front flap. "Does everybody have rain gear?"

Tim replied in the affirmative while the other two men nodded.

"Who's gonna carry what?" Tim asked.

"That's easy," Billy said with great authority. "We each carry our own shit since we all got back packs."

"But what about the tent, and the cooking stuff?" Tim looked at Billy.

"Al carries the tent, it's his." Billy looked at Al and grinned.

"That's fine with me, but." Al pointed to Billy. "He sleeps outside, on the ground," he paused, smiling broadly. "Especially if it's raining, or real cold."

Shaking his head, Billy said, "How 'bout if we take turns caryin' the tent, but Al goes first."

106

"We can divide up all the food we have," John said.

"Should we bring the stove?" Tim asked.

"Naw, we can use a fire better for what we'll have to cook," Al answered. "Besides we can't start it easy, and it weighs too much."

"Well, let's get our gear on, and get going." John leaned over, shoving his feet into his boots.

The others bundled for the rain and cold, then, one by one, crawled out into the cold.

"I gotta take a leak too." Al rushed to the side of the camp site.

"Look," Billy said to the group in general. "I'll start pulling stuff out of the tent, and tearin' it down while y'all empty yourselves."

The four men worked quickly, pulling the equipment out of the green tent, and storing it in backpacks, or leaving it in a pile under a small tarp. They each slung their rifles over their shoulders, under their rain ponchos after they had pulled on their backpacks.

"Let's go, better walk carefully so as not to slide down the bank and into the water," Al warned.

He took the lead as they walked along the bank of the creek, slowly moving down stream. The rain remained steady all that morning. Huge water droplets fell hard on the bare faces of the men while cold water slid from their cheeks and hung from the tips of their noses. Their boots slid slightly as they walked along the water saturated clay and silt of the creek's banks. Where they could, they made a path through the higher ground, but stayed in sight of the flowing water of Harris Creek. All around them, the forest appeared oblivious to the sad weather, the bright glows of late autumn still clung to the trees.

At times a fast moving mist blanketed the forest, the mist thickened between the strongest drizzles. Below their ponchos, their trousers were slowly getting soaked from cold water splashed up from their boots and the driving rain.

"What time is it?" Billy broke the long silence.

107

"Eleven thirty," John answered.

"What say we rest for lunch," Billy said loudly.

The others stopped walking.

"We don't have enough food to eat a nice lunch," Al replied, his body shaking in one short shiver as he stood still.

"I don't give a shit if we don't eat nothin', I need a rest," Billy complained.

"Since you put it that way, I agree," John chimed in.

"Let's not stay still too long," Tim added. "My legs are so cold and tired, I'm afraid they'll cramp up on me if I stop too long. I'll freeze if we don't get going again soon."

Billy nodded and walked to an outcropping of rocks above them, overlooking the creek. He slid his backpack out from under his poncho, and set it on one of the lower rocks, green with moss. He reached into his pack and pulled out a can of pork and beans.

"How about we all eat one can of this stuff?" Billy asked the group.

"Sure." Al walked towards him, pulling out his knife with a can opener on it. He took a spoon out of the side flap of his pack.

The other men took off their back packs and set them next to Billy's. The four of them shared the one can of food in silence.

"How many rounds' you got for your twenty two?" Al looked at Billy.

"I dunno, about four boxes; I guess 'bout two hundred, give or take," Billy answered.

"Keep them dry," Al stated. "That's the only gun we have to shoot small game for food."

"We could shoot a deer and take what we need for one night," Tim said.

"That's against the law, and the law's still the law no matter what condition we're in," Al protested.

"Then why'd we take these heavy rifles?" Tim asked.

"I took mine 'cause it cost a bundle," Billy quickly answered.

"I think that's why we all took 'em," Al added.

"I took mine because it might be the only thing that will keep me alive," John said. "I fought in a real war long enough to know what it takes to stay alive."

"I was there too," Al's voice trailed off. "This don't feel like that, though."

"For some strange reason," John almost whispered to himself. "It does to me."

Tim, the last one to get the can of pork and beans, scraped the bottom of it with the spoon and licked the utensil clean. "Ready to go on?" He tossed the can onto the ground, next to the rock.

"Why? I ain't seen nothin' that looks familiar." Billy stood up.

"I hate to agree with you, but neither have I," Al said. He pointed to the empty can on the ground. "We shouldn't leave our trash here."

"Shit." Tim turned and stared at Al. "Who the fuck cares? Anyway, I don't have the strength to carry all our trash out of here."

"Excuse me." Al shot Tim a worried look as he leaned over and picked up the can.

Al set the can on a large flat rock and flattened it with the heel of his boot then stuffed the flattened can into the large flap on the back of his pack.

"So, what do y'all want to do?" John asked.

"This is starting to give me the creeps," Tim said. "I mean, where are we?"

"Besides being on the West side of Harris Creek, I don't know." Al looked into the dense trees. "We should've passed the crossing about an hour ago, but I didn't see a damn thing, I didn't even see the flat rocks in the creek, not even the first sign of a road."

109

"I told you before, this isn't where, let alone when, we were two days ago," John insisted.

"I know I'm going nuts when I start thinking what he says makes sense." Billy picked up his back pack and began to put it back on under his poncho.

"Don't you start too," Al scolded. "Keep walking down stream and if memory serves me right, the river's not but a few more miles on down there."

"In this weather, that ain't too easy." Tim put his pack on. "Besides, what's so great 'bout the river, ain't the city a good twenty miles up river from there?"

"Yeah, but the river crosses the main road into here, and y'all know how many houses and stores are on that road," Al replied. "Besides, if we head down river, Greensboro is only ten miles or so away."

"I guess so," Billy sighed. "Let's get on with it."

"Billy," Tim said as Al led them back to the creek.

"Yeah?" Billy answered, pausing long enough to make eye contact with him.

"Keep an eye out for dinner," Tim asked, "I'm still hungry."

"You bet." Billy broke into a small grin.

As the afternoon wore on, a thick white fog settled on the forest. They spent most of the rest of daylight struggling through the slick mud, pine needles and leaves next to the creek.

"What you reckon the temperature is?" Billy asked.

"I'd guess it's about thirty to thirty five degrees," John answered.

"That'd be my guess too," Al chimed in.

"Are you worried about hypothermia?" John asked.

"Well, sort'a," Billy answered. "I jest 'member that safety course I took and how they said gettin' wet and cold at the same time could be real dangerous."

"We've got enough rain gear on, and we did drag this damn tent with us to keep dry at night," Al said. "What we have to worry 'bout is how to get to a house, or a store, or some other people."

"What about dinner?" Tim broke into the conversation.

"I don't think there'll be any squirrels out on a day like this." Billy looked up into the trees. "I sure do see a lot of nests, though."

"Naw," Al insisted. "That ain't right, you ain't supposed to shoot up into nests, besides it ain't fair."

"Fair ain't what I'm thinkin'." Billy drew his twenty two pistol from beneath his jacket. "Food is."

"All right." Al held Billy's arm. "I'll throw some rocks up into that low nest, and if one of 'em flushes, then you can get him."

Tim dropped his back pack and threw it against the trunk of a large pine tree, chipping off a chunk of dark brown bark.

"Will you two stop being asses," Tim sounded tired and frustrated.

The three other men looked at each other for a second in silence.

"Look, I'm hungry and don't want no more of your stupid games," Tim paused, sitting on a fallen pine tree, pointing at Al. "You always have to go by the rules, even if they're stupid in this situation, and you." He pointed at Billy, "You always have to be such a big pain in the ass about everything."

Billy flushed; he glanced sideways at Al, stuffed a clip of ammunition into the pistol, and fed a round into the chamber of his Ruger Mark II.

"Throw the damn rock," Billy insisted.

Al scanned over the ground in front of him and selected a medium sized stone, he slipped off his back pack and picked up the stone. He leaned backwards with the stone in his right palm and, with a loud grunt, propelled it to the branch on which the large nest rested while Billy steadied the pistol with both his hands and pointed it at the branch.

Hitting the branch four feet from the nest, the stone made a loud slapping sound; numerous drops of water fell from the entire tree.

Al walked to the fallen stone, picked it up again and wound back up for a more powerful throw. This time the stone struck the bottom side of the nest with the sound of a hollow thump. From a hole in the twigs, two squirrels fell in slow motion. Billy followed them in their earthward flight with the barrel of his pistol. He shot three rounds before the first animal hit the ground; he kept up a rapid fire. Soon two small bodies lay motionless on the forest floor.

"Is that better?" he asked in a sarcastic tone, looking straight into Tim's face.

"Yeah, thanks," Tim said softly.

"It's time to set up for the night, anyway." John took off his back pack. "It's four thirty, and it gets dark real soon out here."

"I shot'em, you clean'em." Billy continued to glare at Tim.

"Fine." Tim walked to the two squirrels, picked them up and strolled to the creek.

As Tim disappeared down the bank to the water, Al looked at John. "What's got him?"

"Fear, it'll get all of us sooner or later," John replied. "Let's get the tent up."

Al walked to his back pack and untied the long tent.

"This' 'bout the heaviest thing any of us got to carry." Al lifted it off his pack. "Someone else's gonna carry it tomorrow."

"We could leave it and use our rain gear as tents." Billy walked to John's pack and removed the tent polls.

"It's too cold for that," John said. "That tent may be the only thing that keeps us from freezing to death at night, especially if it keeps on raining, or worse."

"I agree," Al said. "What's worse, a sore back, or bein' dead?"

"All right," Billy snorted. "I'll carry the damn thing tomorrow, now I'm gonna go look for some more food, if you don't mind." Billy gruffly replied.

"Shit, I don't care, kill as many as you want, however you want," Al sounded indifferent. "I'll help John."

The continuous rain had changed level bare spots on the forest floor into small pools of thick cold mud. They were able to find some cover in a stand of hardwoods and pines. The gray sky grew slowly darker as they two men laid out the tent, connected the fiberglass and aluminum tubing, then strung it through the many fabric loops. As the tent went up, the rain became lighter, almost stopping. At temperatures just above freezing, water can cling to objects with more tenacity; large balls of crystal clear water hung from the branches of every tree, in the still air.

Large billowing clouds of steam hissed from their mouths as they finished setting up the tent. They picked up each of the four back packs, shook the water off them, and set them in the dry tent. Next they stowed all the rifles.

Billy walked slowly into the camp area. "I got a few more, and gave 'em to Tim."

"We heard the shots," Al acknowledged.

"You still got that flint for makin' fires?" Billy asked Al.

"Yeah, I always carry it in my survival can," Al replied.

"Well, start a fire," Billy ordered.

Al looked up at the darkening sky, "The rain's held off for a while, so we'll get a chance to eat a hot meal and get dry before too much longer."

"It ain't stopped rainin' all the way, but let's get started anyway," Billy added. "I wanna see you start a fire with nothin' dry to get it goin'."

"I have faith in him," John said.

"Well okay, so please gather up the driest wood you can find," Al asked.

"Sure," John replied, heading into the woods. "But Tim bothers me, he's usually so calm."

"Don't give him no mind, he's cold and bitchy." Billy squatted down near Al who had started to gather nearby rocks to form a circle on the ground.

While John silently brought over small and large branches, Al cleared inside the circle. He pulled leaves from near the trunks of trees, where they had stayed relatively dry. It was a long process. Eventually Al began shaving thin, curling slivers of wood from a pine branch onto the bed of leaves. Last, he added a pile of brown pine needles to the shavings. Al drew out his flint and striker and began, patiently and slowly, to shoot sparks into the mound of shavings and pine needles.

Finally one of the sparks caught the top of the shavings, which then began to glow a dull red. Al blew softly into the shavings, until a small flame shot out. He quickly formed a little circle of twigs around the smoldering shavings. Al fed more pine needles into the small pile, making the flame grow larger. He fed more pine needles and small twigs into the flames.

"John," Al shouted, not taking his eyes off the growing fire. "John, you got some wood for me?"

"Coming," A voice from the dark forest answered; then John appeared, hurrying up with yet another armful of kindling. Al selected the smallest twigs and continued building larger and larger cones of sticks around the flames. Then he looked up at Billy who had silently been watching the fire grow.

"We need a lot of wood for tonight so go look for an old pine stump and some fat wood so we can get a real good fire goin'."

Without argument, Billy broke himself away from the flames, then disappeared into the forest with John.

At this point, almost at full dark, Tim walked back up from the creek with the five squirrels, cleaned, beheaded and skinned, swinging from his right hand.

"Good, I knew you could get a fire going, if no one else could," Tim paused. "Here's the meat, has anyone gotten a stick to cook it on?"

114

Still feeding the flames, Al said, "I don't know, why don't you look through that pile of wood John brought back?"

Tim pulled a short piece of twine from his pocket, tied the skinned squirrels together and then tied them to a branch of a tree before he walked to the pile of sticks, and began to move them about with his left foot.

"Tim." Al looked up at him for a moment. "What's wrong?"

Tim said nothing, as he poked through the sticks. He looked up into the dark.

"Looks like it'll rain some more," Tim finally said.

"I think so too, but that's not what I asked." Al took a deep breath and let it out slowly. "Somethin's wrong, you don't normally act like that; I know it's a bit frustratin', but we need for everyone to stay calm, and in control."

"I know, but." Tim sat on the ground next to a tree, and leaned against it. "But, nothin's right."

"Talk it out," Al said reassuringly. "Might make both of us feel better."

"Shit, where are we?" Tim's voice rose. "This ain't where we hunted last year, where're all the other hunters? I ain't heard a single shot today, and it's the first week of second huntin' season, and these woods're always crawlin' with nuts like us, shootin' anythin' in sight but I ain't heard jack shit all day." He fell silent.

Al glanced back to the fire, adding another cone of larger sticks around the fire. He had never stopped feeding smaller firewood into the flames.

"I noticed the same thing," Al paused. "I don't know what it means, but we're here and we have keep our wits to get out of here."

"What for? What John says starts to make sense; this might be where we are, but not when. I don't think it's the same time as we were when I wrecked the van." Tim didn't meet Al's eyes.

"Goddamnit, don't you start too; we need to think, not play games with our heads. What he said, can't happen, it can't," Al insisted.

"Good, so you explain it." Tim stood up and walked to the fire.

"If the rain can hold off for a little while longer, the fire'll last long 'nough to cook on," Al said. "Why don't you go get somethin' to cook the meat on?"

"Sure, Al." Tim rested his right hand on Al's shoulder for a second. "I'll be back in a short while."

"Tell the boys to get back here if you see them," Al called as Tim walked into the forest.

"Don't worry, Mom," Billy's voice teased from Al's left.

Billy and John both walked back to the edge of the fire and dumped large arms full of wood onto the dirt.

"That'll be enough," Al said. "I'll start stacking all this wood near the fire so it'll get dry."

"I'll get some water from the creek," Billy replied.

Billy walked to the tent, leaned in and pulled several cooking pots from one of the back packs. He then strolled to the creek, the pots clanking together in his right hand.

John sat next to Al by the fire, grunting as he landed on the ground, "It's been a long day."

"Yeah," Al sniffed. "I talked to Tim while you two were gone."

"I hoped you would, what's wrong?"

"You."

"What does that mean?" John asked.

"You know," Al said. "All your talk 'bout us bein' in another time and all."

"Well, I think we are," John said. "I know what you're going to say, but hear me out."

Al let a deep breath out slowly, "Go on."

"All the other times, I know I was day dreaming, but now I'm not; there's too many things that happen in real life that can't be explained by everyday common sense. For one, the night my

116

father died in a hospital a hundred miles away, that same hour he died, he came to visit us, I saw him, I held his hand and my mom saw him too."

Al stared at John. "And?"

"And, well, he said a few things, then he said he had to go somewhere and that he loved us more than he'd ever told us, then he left. That's what always gives me the strength to look at the world without blinders on. I moved back South, I later quit my job in the city and moved back to the land my family grew up on."

"You ever look back?"

"Back, and front, and all sides." John looked into the forest. "Look over there, do you see anything?"

"What?" Al asked. "The woods?"

"The forest, it's a whole being, and we're part of it now, don't you feel it?"

"What's all this?" Billy walked to the fire with both pots sloshing with water.

"Oh." Al looked up at Billy. "John's tryin' to get me to buy his story 'bout us bein' in another time."

"Well?" Billy asked. "Ain't you buyin' it?"

"Not yet," Al said flatly.

"There's nothing to buy, it's all there, free for the taking." John looked into the fire.

"Do you buy it?" Al asked.

"Sure," Billy replied, "Why not, where's everybody? No shots, no beer cans, no road, no nothin'. If none of that's here, then we must be somewhere else, and we know we ain't, so we must be some time else, ain't that a kick in the ass."

"If everybody else goes crazy, then I'll be the only one to get us out of here," Al complained.

Grimly, Al poked the fire, then added more wood. He began to pile more of the damp wood next to the fire to help dry it off before he added it to the flames.

117

"I said I'm open to all possibilities, Al," John said. "I still want to walk to the river, then up stream to where the road crosses."

"Me too, I ain't dumb," Billy paused. "Maybe I'm goin' crazy, but I ain't dumb."

Tim walked quickly back into camp with several large sticks in his arms.

"We can use these to cook on." Tim handed the sticks to Billy. "You fix it up."

"Yes, sir." Billy snapped to attention, taking the sticks, and bending down next to the fire to set them up to hold the meat.

"I think I can let the fire die down to coals now," Al said.

"There's a good bed of embers to cook over, Al." Tim agreed.

John walked to the tree and untied the pieces of meat.

"I think I saw some smoke rising up, it looked like a camp fire, 'bout two or three miles from here," Tim announced. "We ain't alone, fellas."

"I hope you're right." Al looked in the direction Tim was pointing. "We'll keep an eye out for'em tomorrow, then they'll see our smoke too, before it gets dark."

"Maybe we should try to dry off our boots while the fire is hot, I mean after we eat and before we get into the tent," Al said.

"That's a good idea," John agreed. "Dry them off then knock some of this mud off them too."

Billy rammed a long stick through two carcasses and set it across the supports he had set up on either side of the fire. All four men sat in silence as Billy slowly turned the cooking meat over the fire, which had become a large bed of red embers. Al and Tim fed a few sticks to the fire as the bed of coals died off. Soft sizzling of meat cooking made the most noticeable background noise as the darkness grew over them.

Winds began to blow up the slope, still gentle. Sounds of animals that fed in the day gave way to those of night. What

118

they had decided the night before were wolves started up intermittently; howls pierced the background sounds of smaller animals moving across the forest floor and through the trees.

No words passed during their meal. As they ate the cooked meat and sipped water from the two pots, the chill in the air bit deeper into their flesh. They sat before the fire until John's watch read nine o'clock, when he rose to go to the bathroom in the forest, then disappear into the tent; the others followed, one by one.

The last to linger by the dying fire, Tim waited until it began to rain again, this time mixed with freezing rain and sleet; the cold water hissed as it struck the heated rocks surrounding the fire. He rose and disappeared into the forest, then within ten minutes he reappeared in the fading light of the fire. Tim tossed the other three pairs of drying boots into the tent with him so they wouldn't get soaked.

The rain and freezing rain fell harder, drowning out most other night sounds, the precipitation played a droning tune on the tent roof. The fire faded into cold, black dampness as the thick fog dissipated into frozen drops of water falling from low clouds.

Chapter 13

The wanton Troopers riding by
Have shot my Fawn and it will die.
Ungentle men, They cannot thrive
To kill thee. Thou ne'er didst alive
Them any harm: alas, nor could
Thy death yet do them any good.
Andrew Marvell, The Nymph Complaining for the Death of her Fawn.

The air was icy crisp, fresh, replacing the heavy sensation from the day before as morning light radiated around the large tent.

First to awaken, Al looked at his watch and shook his head. "Hey, wake up y'all."

Billy turned over with his eyes still closed, tasting his tongue. But John immediately sat bolt upright.

"What time is it?" John looked straight ahead, not focused on anybody in the tent.

"Two hours past dawn, almost nine o'clock." Al quickly grabbed his boots from the back of the tent. "We've got to get goin'."

"What we got to eat?" Billy slowly opened his eyes.

"There's a whole forest of food out there, go get you some." Tim sat up, and reached for his boots and coat. "But, I gotta pee first."

Al was the first to leave the tent, untying and pulling back the front flap.

"Will you look at this." Al stood up in front of the tent.

120

Tim followed Al out of the tent, John trailed behind them; they all looked at the thin blanket of snow fallen during the night. Leaves, colored dark brown, red, and yellow, and many scattered limbs and trees stuck through the dusting of white snow, giving the forest floor a mottled look. Ice pellets in the snow made a crunchy texture under their boots.

After relieving himself, Tim walked back to the tent, grabbed the front pole and shook it.

"Get up, we gotta get goin'," he called out.

Billy crawled out of the tent and stretched while Al began to pull the rifles and packs out, laying the rifles on top of each man's pack. John crawled into the tent and pitched several loose items out, then Al began pulling up the tent steaks.

"Let's have at least a can of beans," Billy pleaded.

"We ain't got but five more cans of pork 'n beans, 'n two cans of corn left." Tim answered him. "Besides, I'd puke if I ate beans for breakfast."

"Hell." Billy looked at John with a grin, "Time travel sure makes me hungry."

John looked silently back at Billy for a second, then answered, "I'm going to clean up at the creek."

"What time do ya think we're at?" Billy teased.

"Nine thirty in the morning," John replied flatly.

"Look." Billy lost his grin. "I don't wanna bust my ass like I did yesterday. I'm hungry, still tired, 'n my back's killin' me from yesterday 'n it's my day to carry the goddamn tent."

"I know, I tied the tent to your pack," Al interrupted. "And I put the poles on John's."

"Come on, boys, let's not kill each other until we get out of this." John trudged back from the creek..

"I agree," Tim added. "Let's all look at where we are, 'n try to figure out what's goin' on."

"I wasn't kidding, I believe John. We're in some other place or time since this forest sure ain't the forest I know." Billy looked around at the tall trees.

"Explain that?" Tim asked, cocking his head slightly and looking at Billy.

"Look at it, does it look familiar?"

Al cleared his throat, "It does to me, I've been comin' to this place since my father first took me here forty five years ago, it looks the same to me."

"How?" Billy asked indignantly. "Look out there, I see trees I ain't seen here before." He pointed to his left. "Look at that one, what the hell is it?"

"It's a chestnut tree," John answered.

"Can't be," Al insisted.

"I taught botany one year. That's a chestnut tree and I've seen them around us since early yesterday," John stated. "American chestnut trees, a whole lot of them too; look at the nuts on the ground."

"It's like a stranger," Billy said quietly. "I mean, this creek's too big, the lay of the land looks the same, but there's too many hardwoods, 'n not enough pines, plus there's too many little critters runnin' around."

"If this ain't the National Forest, and, if this is some other time," Tim asked. "Then who the hell made that fire I saw last night?"

"If our imaginations run away from us, all we'll do is sit here 'n tell ghost stories all day," Al huffed. "We can scare the shit out of each other on the trail if y'all want to, but let's get goin' now."

Al stuffed his rain gear and a few small items into his pack and pulled it over his shoulder, sniffed then walked briskly away.

The other three men struggled to pull their gear on their backs before they grudgingly caught up with Al who had already walked to the edge of the creek.

"The fire I saw last night." Tim pointed over his shoulder. "It came from back that-a-way."

"How far?" Billy asked, catching a breath.

"I don't know," Tim answered. "It's hard to judge distances in the woods, 'specially at dusk."

"I've noticed that," John chimed in. "It looks like you can see a long way through all these trees, but you can't; it appears like there's a lot of area in any given tract like this." John spread his hands. "But, your eyes are deceived."

"What the hell are you talkin' 'bout?" Al asked. "You can see twenty acres or more from right here."

"You can't make out a small detail, like another man, or a two hundred pound buck, at much more than one hundred yards in this heavy a forest," John said.

Al paused for a moment as he turned to look back at John before he spoke, "I guess you're right."

"Anyway," Tim continued. "I don't care how far away they was, I saw the fire, and smelled the smoke from another campfire last night."

"All that means is we're not alone, 'n we'll run across someone today for sure," Al grunted.

"What if we don't?" Billy asked.

"Then, we keep walking until we find people," John answered.

"Smart ass," Billy whispered under his breath.

As their pace quickened and their breathing became heavier, conversation turned sparse. After walking for forty five minutes, the four men halted and looked at each other.

"What the hell's this?" Billy demanded.

"It's a swamp, stupid," Tim answered, wrinkling his face slightly as he glared at Billy.

"I can see that," Billy said in an annoyed voice. "But, where the hell is it?"

"You got a point," Al said. "This can't be the Harris Creek, there ain't never been no swamp this big on it."

"So what now?" Tim demanded.

The forest had thinned inside a one to three foot band next to the creek, where a carpet of pine needles and dead leaves made walking soft but sometimes slick. They had been looking at

123

this landscape for at least the last day. Also, for the last day and a half, they had followed a clear, well defined animal trail next to the creek. They could always observe, by this path, the easiest way through any obstacles, and around forks in the creek.

But what lay ahead of them, a large marshy body of water, defied their efforts to see around it. They found an expanse of deeper water where beaver had blocked off the creek, but they could not see more of the swamp from their present vantage point.

Al turned to face the other three, "What the hell do we do now?"

"You're the expert." Tim shook his head. "What do you think?"

"I'm not an expert, but I say we try to skirt this mess," John said. "The creek's got to continue on the other side of all this so if we stay to the edge of this swamp, we should get to the creek again, then the river."

"That sounds more logical than anything you've come up with so far," Billy replied. "Let's do it."

Al, scratching his chin, looked hard at John. "I guess I'll have to agree with you this time." He then looked at Tim. "What do you think?"

"Let's go," Tim replied.

Al began to climb off the path, up the steep incline leading from the creek. Digging in with their boots, the men made it to the crest of a ridge overlooking the creek.

Tim pointed to the center of the swamp, "Look, see the pond in the middle of all that? It's a big one and I'll bet there's fish in it."

Billy agreed, "That'll taste better than beans for lunch."

"Stop 'n think," Al insisted. "What're you gonna use for a hook and line, 'n how're you gonna get to that pond through all that muck around it?"

"What a buzz kill," Billy sighed. "I'll think on it, 'n let you know."

124

"Good," Al added. "This ridge follows the edge of the swamp so let's go on for a while."

Al began walking due west into the thick, pathless forest; the others turned from the view of the small lake, and followed him.

"Let's all keep an eye to our left," Al turned to say. "That swamp's our only reference point, so don't lose it."

Walking was a much slower process than it had been along the creek's edge. Fallen limbs, small seedlings, and enormous, tall bushes blocked their way. Up here, dry grasses rattled in the cool breeze like a Spring rattlesnake waking up. They carefully negotiated the ground to avoid tripping or stepping into a hole left by a rotted stump. No fallen tree was cut by man, although many had been gnawed down by beavers. The same abundance of wildlife existed in the swamp as had existed near the creek.

Al stopped the others with a motion of his arm.

"Look," Al whispered. "Look toward that fallen tree up there."

Tim nodded his head, straining to see beyond it, "I see some deer."

"Some?" Al asked with a tinge of incredulity. "Look harder, and to the right."

"There must be a hundred of 'em," Billy whispered.

"I ain't never seen so many in one place in my life," Al sounded amazed. "Either John's right, or we found the best damned huntin' spot in the country."

"Let me get one of 'em." Billy quietly lowered his back pack to the ground.

He slowly slipped several cartridges from his pocket and began to load his rifle.

"What the hell for?" Tim asked. "We can't eat it all?"

"I could make a big damned dent in one, myself."

Billy raised his rifle to his shoulder and looked in the direction of the deer through his telescopic sight.

125

Al put is hand on the barrel of Billy's rifle, and pushed it towards the ground. "Don't do it, it ain't right to kill somethin' less we're gonna use it."

"Let him do it," John interrupted. "We'll eat it."

"If you shoot it now, we'll be stuck here for hours, dressin' it, 'n cuttin' the meat up," Al said. "Why don't you wait 'till later, that way we could get a bit farther along before we have to stop."

"What if there ain't no more deer up there?" Billy asked.

"We've seen deer 'n every kind of small eatin' game almost every foot of the way for two days, I wouldn't worry 'bout it," Al answered.

"I think Al's got a point," John said.

"But, shit," Billy whispered loudly. "Look through my scope at that herd."

Billy handed his rifle to John, who looked through the scope at the deer ahead.

"I ain't never seen nothin' like it in my whole life, 'n I might never get a chance like this again," Billy insisted.

"That is a nice big one." John looked through the scope. "It looks like twelve, or fourteen points, it also looks like it weighs well over two hundred pounds."

John lowered the rifle, and handed it back to Billy.

"We're after food, not a trophy so one of the smaller does would be better," John added.

"It ain't a doe day," Al protested in a whisper with a hurt look growing over his face.

"I don't think we're where it matters," John observed.

"There you go again with that shit," Al retorted in a loud voice.

At once, the deer broke cover and rushed away from their gathering spot. Several remained for a brief moment, snorting loudly They also scattered in different directions while the men watched.

"Well, forget 'em." Billy angrily unloaded his rifle and pulled his pack back over his shoulders.

126

"It looked like forty or so to me," Tim calmly said.

"So many deer, and no shots anywhere," John sounded puzzled.

"So?" Al said indignantly.

"So," John paused. "Why not?"

"I don't know, 'n that bothers me," Al's voice became louder. "But what bothers me most, is your shit; keep it to your self, will ya."

"Calm down, Al." Billy quietly put his hand on Al's arm. "Take it like I do," he paused. "I believe him, but I'm still walkin' my way outta here; if he's right, that's okay, spooky, but okay but if he ain't, that's okay too."

"I think I believe him too," Tim added. "I'm scared it's true."

"I don't mean to terrify anybody," John spoke up. "All I'm doing is observing what's around me, I'm not letting my brain tell me what I see, I'm looking at what I see."

"What the hell're you talking 'bout this time?" Billy asked.

"We're not walking through this forest, we're in it, we've been part of it for the last few days," John paused, looking at the others. "All the past times I've been on trips with you guys, this feeling's been with me, that's why I used to pretend I was in another time. For me, it demonstrated the timelessness of these surroundings; we all belong to the land, and this forest is the closest to what land has been for man during his entire history on this planet."

"So?" Al looked blankly into John's face.

"So, we're lost in a place and in a time," John answered. "Drop your pretenses and concentrate on where you are and what you need to do to survive."

"Why didn't you say that in the first place?" Al sounded indignant.

"I did." John shrugged his shoulders.

"I ain't droppin' my pretenses for none of you queers." Billy looked from face to face, waiting for a reaction to his lame pun.

127

"Try dropping dead." John turned away from Billy.

"It wasn't that bad a joke," Tim added.

"Let's get on with it," Al said.

Al began walking along the ridge again, with the others following behind. They walked in silence for another two hours as one ridge gave way to another, each giving the men a clear view of the swamp and a series of ponds and small lakes; the sun sparkled off the almost still water. The remaining leaves displayed the bright but fading colors of late Fall withering into a Southern winter. As they trudged on, the breeze was slight and cool on their faces. But by one o'clock that afternoon, none of the snow had melted from the ground.

The forest became more intense in its undergrowth, the land became less hilly and the ridges disappeared into more and more flat, swampy sections. This area had a multitude of small branches of shallow, clear water, all running in the same general direction.

"Look at the water level marks on those trees." Al pointed to a stand of hardwoods to his left.

"Yeah, but I don't hear no river." Billy stopped and cocked his head.

"Could be we're near the river, though." Tim also stopped. "You know how the water marks are higher on the trees near to the river, showin' when it floods."

"It could also be that the beaver dams break on a regular basis." John stopped and slipped off his back pack. "There could be ten more miles of this crap before we get to the river."

"You've got nothing but good news, don't you," Billy said.

"I'm realistic, that's all," John answered. "Anyway, I'm getting tired of walking."

"You want to stop here for the day?" Al asked.

"Not here." John pointed to a small rise. "Over there."

"Sounds good," Billy replied. "I'm gonna hunt some meat now."

128

"Don't shoot in our direction," Al cautioned him. "And mark your trail goin' out so you can find your way back here."

"Yes, mommy," Billy mockingly said.

"Somebody needs to keep you alive," Al growled back at him.

"Come on over 'n help put the tent up," Tim called to Al, who turned toward the half constructed tent as Billy walked back along the trail the four of them had trampled down. John walked into a thicker portion of the nearby forest, looking intently at the ground.

"What 'bout water, Al?" Tim asked.

"It's right over there." Al pointed to the swamp and a shallow, slow moving branch.

"I ain't gonna drink that stuff."

"Boil it."

"Yeah, I forgot." Tim said sheepishly.

"Damn it," Al sighed. "Can't you turkeys do one damn thing on your own, do I have to do all your thinkin'?"

From his pockets, John emptied a large amount of chestnuts into the tent.

"You don't have to do all the thinking for us, in fact, you've done only one fourth of it for us so far," John observed.

"But every time I turn around I have to straighten up one of you," Al insisted.

"Not each time, and sometimes we straighten you up," John replied.

"What does that mean?" Al said loudly, stepping back a pace. "I want to know."

"Calm down, Al," Tim said. "We all need to get along, 'n we need each other."

"Tim said it." John sat on the ground, crossing his legs and cracking the nuts with two stones. "All I was saying was that all four of us got a common goal, getting out of here alive."

As Al stood over John, looking down at him, a loud shot echoed through the forest. An animal cried out then fell silent. The silence stretched on, as if the whole forest held its breath.

129

Billy proudly marched up to the freshly killed deer; it was a one shot kill. He had settled into the crotch of a large red oak for less than five minutes before a large buck and four smaller does sauntered by. He was no more than thirty yards from the doe he mentally chose to kill when he took aim and fired his rifle. He nudged the deer carcass with the barrel of his rifle to make sure it was dead. He leaned his seven millimeter magnum against the nearest tree, then took in a deep breath as he pulled out his knife from the pouch hanging on the right side of his belt; time to butcher the deer and begin hauling the meat back to camp. But Billy thought someone should help him.

"Hey, mister," a voice from not far away shouted. "Did you get a buck?" It sounded like a teenage boy.

"Who's that," Billy shouted. "Is that one of you?" John or Tim's voice might sound like that coming through the woods but not Al's; his voice was too deep and gravely.

"It's me," The voice immediately answered. "It's Mark Rose from down by the mill."

The voice came from the south somewhere. Billy shook his head, he had a clear memory of finding no signs of strangers for miles around this spot. He wondered if one of his friends had circled around him while he was shooting the deer.

"What mill?" Billy stood up on his tip-toes since he couldn't see a thing in any direction.

"'Bout a mile or so up the river from here," the person who called himself Mark Rose answered.

The river? Billy hadn't seen the river yet the river might be close.

"We're lost out here," Billy shouted back. "Can you help us find the town?"

"Sure thing," The young voice answered. "Where are you now?"

130

"I can't hear you," Billy shouted, realizing that he was loosing track of the only new human he had heard in over two days. "You must be walking away from me."

"I ain't gone nowhere." The voice was almost gone, it was as if whoever had been there was running away. "Hello."

"Where did you go," Billy shouted as loud as he could.

"Hey, mister." The voice was fading even more. "Hey mister, we'll send someone back later." The voice was now almost indistinguishable from the background woodland noises.

. . . .

John whispered, looking up at Al, "Never realized how many animal sounds we can hear until they stop. Listen to how quiet everything is since Billy fired his rifle."

"Yeah." Al turned to face the direction of the shots. "I wonder if someone should help Billy bring the animal back here?"

"Why don't you go help him?" Tim asked.

Al didn't answer, he pulled several items from his pack and then ambled down the path Billy had taken, "Billy, I'm comin' to help, did ya get somethin'?"

"Yeah," the answer loudly reverberated. "Did you guys hear that kid?"

"What kid?" Al looked at Tim, then at John.

"Beats me," Tim sounded confused. "Maybe you'd better go on out there and see what's his problem, I'll get some more of those nuts, they look good."

"Wait, I'll go with you, but let me look for a bag or something to carry them in," John said.

He stood up and walked to his back pack, reached into it and pulled out an undershirt. Tying the neck and arm openings, he proudly displayed the sack he had made. Together they gathered food from under the chestnut trees as they walked, but only a short distance down the trampled path Al spotted Billy, standing by a doe.

131

"Dead?" Al asked loudly.

"Dead as they get," Billy replied with a large grin. "This kill was damned easy, it was the best shot I've ever had at one of these white tailed devils since I started huntin'."

"What were you asking about a kid for" Al asked.

"I don't want to get you goin' again, but I heard this voice out there callin' me," Billy answered. "I think there's people not far from here."

Al gave him a confused look.

"Someone called to me 'n asked if I got a buck," Billy assured Al. "He said there's a town not far from here 'n he'd help get us there."

"So, where is he?" Al looked around the swampy woods. "Maybe we should go look for him."

"It's almost dark," Billy interrupted.

"I guess you're right." Al took in a deep breath. "What else did he say?"

"He said somethin' about a mill about a mile from here, up river."

"Up river?" Al looked at Billy. "How far away's the river from here?"

"He didn't say," Billy sounded annoyed. "He ran away before I could ask him."

"Why did he run away?" Al asked.

"How the hell do I know." Billy said, still annoyed. "Why don't you find him and ask him yourself."

"Which way did his voice come from?" Al said, somewhat anxiously. He wanted answers he could deal with.

"From the south, the same way we walked here from," Billy muttered, looking at the deer on the ground and wanting desperately to change the subject. "Look, we'd better get started here before we lose all the light."

"Okay, we can tell the others when we get back, let's get to it," Al said.

Al pulled a long knife from under his coat and walked to the deer. Billy lifted the front right leg of the animal up and

132

made a shallow cut with his knife into the upper abdomen. He then cut slowly upwards; blood oozed from the puncture, following the direction of the upward cut. Billy then reached into the now opened chest cavity and cut the esophagus from within the body. He continued the cut down to the anus and circled it with a deep cut. Rolling the lifeless doe belly down, the internal organs fell onto the forest floor.

"Want to quarter it?" Al asked.

"Might be the best way, but shouldn't we skin it first?"

"What for?" Al asked. "We wanna eat it, we ain't gonna wear it, ya know."

"Guess not." Billy reached for Al's large knife. "But, it'll make it easier later when we go to cook it, so let's skin it."

Al passed his knife and small hatchet to him and watched as Billy hacked the carcass into four pieces. He first cut it in half along the backbone, then he by cut through the bottom of the rib cage. Billy and Al then cut off the skin from the quarters.

Al took one of the quarters and began to cut large pieces of meat off, placing them on the ground.

"We can wash the meat in the water over there." Billy pointed with a bloody finger to a small, shallow flow of water.

"I hate to use such scummy lookin' water to clean it, but I guess since we'll cook the stuff anyway, it'll be all right," Al said.

Tim and John returned to camp first, and began cracking nuts with large rocks, putting the nut meat into the largest cooking pot. As they finished shelling the last of the chestnuts, Al and Billy walked into camp, carrying large chunks of freshly slaughtered meat.

"Soup's on." Billy proudly held up a large piece of red meat.

"I hope you plan to cook it first," Tim remarked.

"Yeah, 'n you two ought to build a big damn fire pretty soon, like right now," Billy said.

"Hang that stuff up, 'n help us gather wood," Tim said.

Billy heard someone out there callin' to him," Al said.

"Who?" John quickly turned to face Billy.

133

"I thought it was one of you guys at first," Billy replied, motioning for John to take some of the hunks of meat from him. "But it was some kid named Mark somethin'."

"Where's his house?" John took two large pieces of deer meat from Billy. "How far away is he?"

"Back off, bubba," Billy snorted. "Like I told Al, he didn't say that much before he ran away."

"What did he say?" Tim asked.

"He said there's a mill about a mile up the river, and that his name's Mark somethin' and that he'd try to help us," Billy answered.

"Do you remember his last name?" John quickly asked. "It might be important."

"How the hell could that be important?" Billy flashed an annoyed look at John.

"I'd like to know that too." Tim fashioned a flat surface out of several larger branches so that the other men could put the meat down without getting it in the dirt.

"I don't know." John vaguely asked. "I suppose it could be of some use."

"I suppose it's too dark to try 'n go chasing after whoever it was." Al put his portions of deer meat on the home-made table. "We could pick up a trail tomorrow."

"Yeah," Billy added. "I think the voice came from the south, the same way we came from."

"You mean we walked the wrong way from where the van wrecked?" Tim sounded quite perplexed. "I can't believe that."

"We saw a campfire last night," John said. "Billy heard someone talking to him tonight;   I think we'll find civilization tomorrow for sure."

"I hope you're right." Al dug in his pack for his fire starting materials.

"Let's keep an eye out for more camp fires tonight," Tim added. "We could walk that way tomorrow."

134

All four men spent the next hour gathering a large pile of wood for Al to start another fire. Once the fire grew high enough, Billy cut the fresh meat into strips while Tim wandered through the immediate forest, looking for proper cooking stakes. Each man took handfuls of nuts to munch on while doing their tasks.

"Keep 'n eye on the fire," Al asked John. "Me 'n Billy have to clean up and get all this blood off us."

"Yeah, let's try 'n find some deep, clean water near here; I don't want to get lost in this dark swamp, that's for sure." Billy said, following Al towards the swamp.

John stared at the fire, feeding it sticks once in a while. Tim walked into camp with several large sticks, and began to make the cooking rack for the meat.

"When you get it up, start cooking the meat," John said.

"Sure."

"I wish I'd told my wife to check on me earlier," John sighed.

"What're you talkin' 'bout?"

"I wish I'd brought my cell phone with me," John replied.

"Me too, but we've only got one, and I left that for my wife," Tim said. "But, what are you driving at?"

"I told her that I wouldn't be back, or call her for five days," John paused, then stood up to stretch. "If I'd said I'd call her in two days, or the day after we got here, maybe she'd have come out looking for us by now."

"She'd never find us out here, besides I thought you said we were in another time?"

"Yes, but we might also be still be in the wreck, unconscious and dreaming all this, at least she could wake us up," John replied.

"You've been thinkin' that too?" Tim asked. "I didn't want to say nothin' because it'd piss Al off even more."

"You're right about that," John agreed. "So, you too think we may be unconscious back at the wreck."

135

"Or, we could be dead," Tim answered.

"Not a pleasant thought."

"But as valid as the alternative," Tim said. "Is this heaven, or is this hell?"

"Tim." John's eyes opened wider. "Sometimes you surprise me."

"You didn't answer me."

"What?"

"If we died in the crash, where are we?"

"In the forest, somewhere, some time," John answered. "What makes you think that we're dead?"

Tim looked puzzled for a second, then spoke, "All I remember is the van startin' to crash; I felt a lot of pain, then I don't remember nothin' until you woke me up."

"So?" John shrugged. "I'm not St. Peter, and these aren't the pearly gates."

"Yeah, but this strange place spooks me," Tim said. "And, I can't help thinkin' 'bout why we're here. And, I haven't got a clue."

John sighed. "All we can do is continue to think, perhaps the answer will come."

"This all feels so real." Tim looked around the camp site.

"Oh, it is," John agreed. "Even if we're dreaming this, it's still real because I feel cold and hungry and my legs are cramping from too much walking."

"You know what I'm getting at," Tim insisted. "What if we're all dead or knocked out back there at the crash?"

"It's been two days, if we're out in the cold and snow, how long can we last?" John paused. "But, I know what you mean."

"I'm glad somebody does." Tim laughed a little. "I'm not sure I know what I mean."

"Whose dream is this?" John looked serious.

"What?"

"If we're all unconscious, it's unlikely we're all having the same dream, so whose point of view is this?" John asked.

136

"I guess I see your point," Tim paused. "We all are experiencing the same thing, so we're all in it together, whatever it is."

"Maybe." John looked at the fire, then added a few more medium sized sticks. "All of us are the same as when we left home two days ago, but this forest sure isn't."

"Like I said before." Tim slowly took in a breath. "What if we're dead and this forest is really the waiting room for us four until someone decides if we go up or down?"

"I hate to admit it, but I think Billy has the best idea," John chuckled. "We could be in another time, or another place, however we all have no choice but to look for a way out of this forest."

"But I can't help thinkin' this is some kind of a test for us, like, are we good 'nough for heaven?"

"You're back on that?" John asked.

"I can't get it out of my mind, that's all."

"So, where do you think we are?" John asked, cocking his head.

"I don't rightly know, could be hell."

"We each have our own hells to endure, some of us face them like this, others think they never face them, but all of us have to eventually."

"What do you mean?" Tim asked sharply.

"Nothing, keep those thoughts to yourself and cook the deer meat." John sat back down on the ground next to the fire. "Al has enough trouble with all this already, so let's not confuse him beyond all reason."

The two men continued their tasks. Soon they were watching two hunks of meat searing over the fire.

"Fire needs to go down a bit," Tim said.

John nodded and lay back against a short log he had dragged into camp.

"It's going to be cold tonight," John paused. "A hell of a lot colder than last night."

"I'd rather be cold than cold and wet."

137

"You said the truth."

Al and Billy walked back into camp together, a little cleaner than before.

"We found a pond up there, 'n the water's runnin' through it pretty good," Al said. "We ought to get some pots of water from it for tonight; we can boil it clean over the fire."

"I can take a hint." John got up and walked to the tent, reached inside and pulled out two pots. "Where is this running water?"

Billy pointed to his left, "Follow the path Al 'n I made, Ya can't miss it."

"Be careful, it's a tad muddy," Al added.

Billy asked Tim, "How's it goin'?"

"It's cookin'," Tim answered. "Maybe we ought to cook all of it, that way we can take what we don't eat."

"That's what we was talkin' 'bout while we was cleanin' up." Al added.

"Did either of you tell anyone you were gonna call before we was to get back?" Tim paused a short while. "John 'n I was talkin' 'bout that; he said he should've told his wife he was gonna call the day after we got here, that way they would already be lookin' for us by now. Did you tell Darlene where you'd be, or tell her you'd call her?"

"Hell no, she don't care a lick no way," Billy answered.

Tim looked up at Billy, surprised, "Don't say that. Darlene's a nice girl, 'n she loves you a lot, don't always be puttin' her down."

"What's it to you, anyway?" Billy sat down next to the other two men. "She ain't nothin' to you."

"She 'n Billy Jean get together 'n talk their heads off," Tim said.

"So, what they got to talk 'bout?" Billy interrupted.

"You," Tim said softly. "Darlene don't like the way you treat her."

Billy became red in the face and spoke in a loud, belligerent voice, "That's none of your damn business, that's a

138

private thing 'tween me 'n my wife, 'n your 'ol whore oughtta keep her goddamn nose outta it."

"Now, Billy." Al tried to calm Billy down. "Keep your temper, we all know how you can get sometimes."

Tim looked down at Billy with a mean squint, "My wife's no whore, you watch what you say, you son of a bitch, or I'll stomp you worse than you ever stomped Darlene."

Billy stood up and faced Tim closely with grave intensity.

"You're gonna do what?" Billy demanded.

Al quickly wedged himself between the them.

"Look, both of you calm down and you watch your temper, Billy," Al pleaded.

Al pushed them away from each other, hoping for the best.

"Look you ol' fagot, you wouldn't know what to do with a woman anyway, so stay outta this fight between two real men," Billy hissed at the older man.

"That does it," Tim rasped out.

He thrust his right foot into Billy's groin, who crumpled over and shouted in pain. Tim spun quickly to his left, raising his right foot back up, striking the side of Billy's head and knocking him unconscious.

"You didn't kill him, did you?" Al asked.

"I shut him up," Tim replied, breathing hard as he sat back down next to the fire. "He should be back with us in an hour or two."

Al sat silently back down by the fire and stared at the flames. Just then, John reappeared with two pots of water.

"Should I ask what happened?" John asked, looking at Billy's crumpled form.

"I beat the crap out of our loud mouth friend," Tim said, looking at the fire.

"Why?"

"I brought up Darlene," Tim paused. "And, one thing led to another."

"You should know better," John observed.

139

"I don't give a damn, he treats his wife like shit, 'n I don't think that's right. She's intelligent, beautiful, and has a figure that puts Miss America to shame, she deserves better."

"Meaning you?" John asked.

"Don't you start too," Tim said, an edge to his voice.

"Hey." John made a broad upward sweep of his arms, as if to fend off something. "I know you have a black belt, and I'm not that stupid."

"That ain't it," Tim sighed.

"All I'm saying is, that you might be identifying with Darlene too much, and if you get too deep into their problems, they might become yours," John said, sitting down on the ground near Billy.

"Yeah, yeah, I guess you're right, but he also worked over Al pretty bad."

"I don't see any blood." John cast a quick glance at Al.

"He called him a fagot."

Al looked up at John. "I ain't no fagot, I know what everybody says, but I ain't no fagot; 'cause I ain't never got married, don't mean I'm no fagot."

"Nobody thinks that, Al," John said calmly.

"That's a bunch of shit, I know what they all say behind my back," Al mumbled.

"We're your friends, 'n we know you ain't no fagot." Tim put his hand on Al's shoulder.

"I thought Billy was my friend too." Al's expression was grim and bleak.

"You know how Billy talks without thinking," John said quietly. "His mouth works with no connection to his brain at all when he gets mad; he'll fall all over himself apologizing when he comes to."

Al broke into a small smile, which quickly disappeared, "I ain't never even thought 'bout doin' none of that queer stuff."

The three men sat in silence as Tim cooked the meat over the fire, placing the finished pieces in the unused metal pots. Al walked to the tent and retrieved an extra pot, put a piece of

140

cooked meat in it, and walked away from the fire to eat it. John and Tim ate by the fire in silence.

As the sun set and the darkness grew, John poured a cup of water from the pot on the side of the fire. He brought it to Al who silently took it, nodding his head in appreciation. John poured two more cups of water for himself and Tim. He then walked to Billy and slowly poured the cool pot of water over Billy's head; Billy gradually regained consciousness, grunting a few times.

"We know you're still alive, so get your ass up," John said. He continued to slowly pour water onto Billy's face.

Billy sat up abruptly and looked all around, focusing on the fire, then on Al, sitting fifty yards away on a fallen tree trunk.

"How long have I been out?" he asked.

"A little over an hour; I thought you should get up, eat something, then go back to sleep," John replied.

"Did that son of a bitch knock me out?" Billy pointed towards Tim, who was staring into the flames.

"Yes, and I'd watch what I said to him in the future, he does have a black belt in karate you know," John said. "Is anything broken?"

Billy stroked the side of his face and chin, "I don't think so; some day I'm gonna kick his ass all over the place."

"But not now," John insisted. "We have to act semi-grown up, at least until we're out of here. We each need each other to survive, so pack your hostility up and act human for a while longer."

Billy took in a deep breath and held it for a second, then let it out slowly, "I know I can get a little mad once 'n a while, but I don't like people tellin' me how to live my life."

"The rest of us don't like you telling us how to think, and insulting us," John said deliberately.

"I don't tell nobody how to think," Billy protested.

"Yes you do." John gave him a harsh glance. "You also hurt Al's feelings and I think you ought to say something to him."

"What?"

"Don't you remember, you called him a fagot," John said.

"Oh, yeah," Billy paused. "But everybody does."

"I don't and neither does Tim."

"Well, la-te-da, ain't you the do gooders," Billy teased.

"No, we're his friends, and I thought you were too."

"Yeah, I guess I am, kind of." Billy slowly stood up and shook his head. "I'm gonna get that son of a bitch some time for good."

"If you keep trying, you may get yourself killed."

Billy looked at John and chuckled, "I guess you're right," he paused, still rubbing the side of his head. "I guess it's better to be his friend anyway."

"That's the spirit," John chuckled.

Billy walked to the fire and stuck his hand in Tim's direction.

"I'm sorry I got mad at ya," Billy apologized.

Tim and Billy shook hands. Billy then walked to Al, who didn't look at him.

Billy shoved his hand towards Al, "I'm real sorry I said what I did, I didn't mean it."

Al kept looking at his empty plate. He lifted his water cup and took a shallow sip from it then slowly put it back on the ground; Billy kept his hand extended to Al.

"You know how I don't know what I'm sayin' when I get in one of my bad moods," Billy paused for a second. "You remember that time in the bar on the highway, that 'ol guy I mouthed off to?"

"Yeah, he beat the shit outta you then, too," Al replied. "Maybe you should've learned by now."

Billy laughed as he rubbed the side of his head, "Yeah, maybe I should've."

Al stood and extended his hand to Billy.

"I didn't mean to hurt you none, Al," Billy said.

"I know you didn't," Al said, and sighed.

142

Billy and Al stood, looking awkwardly at each other then Al returned to the fire, and sat on a rock near the warmth. All four men sat by the fire while Al fed wood into it.

"It's gonna be colder than a witch's tit tonight," Billy said.

"It already is," Tim added. "I'll bet it's in the twenties already, what time is it?"

"Eight thirty," Al answered.

"Let's keep the fire goin' as long as we can." John rubbed his hands together in front of the fire.

"I wonder if we can see any other fires out there?" Tim asked.

"Why don't you go look," Billy suggested.

"I will," Tim responded.

Tim stood, shoved his hands in his coat pockets and walked from the flickering light of the fire.

"What if he finds somethin'?" Al asked. "What if he finds that kid from the mill?"

"I ain't goin' out in the dark to look for 'em," Billy said.

"Let's wait for Tim, but I bet no one's out there tonight," John said.

Tim quickly walked back to the fire and sat down.

"Well?" Al asked.

"I saw the campfire out there again." Tim pointed to the west. "This time it's closer; go on out that way for a little bit, 'n you can smell their fire, the wind's blowin' from that direction."

"What're they havin' for dinner?" Billy asked, still looking at the fire.

"Why don't you go on out there 'n find out," Tim still sounded angry at Billy.

"Let's try to find them tomorrow," John interrupted. "I'd hate to get lost even more in the dark, besides it's too cold now to do something that stupid."

"Yeah," Al agreed. "As soon as we run across some other people we'll find out if John's right or crazy like usual."

John laughed as he looked back into the fire which crackled and hissed as he added green and wet wood to it. The

143

flames consumed the wood, and the concentration of the four men as they sat on the ground, as close to the heat as was comfortable, staring at the quickly changing patterns of the red to blue flames.

"I sure miss my old lady," Tim said with a sigh.

"Don't look at me, you weirdo," Billy teased. "I don't care 'bout your karate, you come near me tonight, 'n you're a dead man."

"That's not what I meant," came the annoyed retort.

"I miss Janice right now, and not for the reason you think," John said.

"All right." Billy shook his head. "Maybe I'm the only one here who know what's good for him."

"And." John glared at Billy. "Maybe you're not."

"I miss her company," Tim spoke up. "I mean, you guys are okay, and I need to be with guys on trips like these."

"Not like these," Al interrupted.

"Well," Tim continued. "I meant like a normal hunting trip, but I sure miss her voice and her touch after a few days."

"I know the feeling." John looked at the camp fire. "Ever since I first saw Janice, I wanted to be with her and listen to her, and make love to her for the rest of my life."

"What did she think of you, the first time she saw you?" Al asked.

"What the hell is this, the damned Newlyweds Game?" Billy stirred the coals of the fire with a long stick.

"Shut up," Tim abruptly said, looking at Billy with a hard gaze. "I want to hear this too."

John took a long, deep breath and continued, "Janice thought I was a geek, she gave me the coldest look I'd ever seen when I tried to start a conversation. I remember meeting her for the first time at a reception after a concert, it was at the college we both went to. We both dressed to the hilt, and neither of us had a steady at the time."

"Does that mean you wasn't gettin' none?" Billy smirked.

144

"All that means is that we were both in the market," John said, ignoring him. "At first she wanted no part of me for any kind of a relationship, even though we found out that first evening that both of our families came from this area."

"How long did it take to work her resistance down?" Tim smiled at him. "Billy Jean 'n I met in high school, 'n we always liked each other. There ain't never been a time we ain't been together or didn't want to be together."

"I wish Janice and I could have had such a beginning," John paused. "It took a long time to become friends with her, then to become lovers."

"You two seem like such a good couple," Al said. "You both look like you've been together forever."

John fell silent, gazing into the flames.

"Me 'n Billy Jean planned our weddin' since the ninth grade, I ain't never thought of no other woman since then." Tim looked into the fire.

"I knocked Darlene up when we both was seniors in high school," Billy spoke up. "And, well, that was that."

"How romantic." John looked sideways at him.

"It ain't supposed to be romantic, that's the point," Billy insisted.

"That might be my problem," John sighed.

"What's your problem?" Billy asked.

"Expecting too much out of a marriage."

"What's to expect?" Billy shrugged his shoulders. "A piece of ass when you want, 'n someone to tell you what a jerk you are when you don't deserve it."

"Go to a whore house for a piece," Tim grumbled, looking into the flames. "And I'll tell you what a jerk you are any time you want."

"What did you mean?" Al asked, looking at John.

"Why do you ask?" John turned towards Al.

"Sounds like you might be having problems with Janice," Al inquired.

145

"No, not anymore," John answered. "It's more that I always give more involvement than the other person is willing to accept in any relationship, and I always want more from it than they're willing to give."

"Are you screwin' around?" Billy looked at John.

"No, that's not the only definition of a relationship," John answered.

"Well?" Billy asked. "What are you doin'?"

"Sitting in front of the fire with three other men, lost in the forest, somewhere," John answered.

"Funny," Billy muttered.

They were all were silent for a brief period before Al looked up at John and spoke, "You said that Janice came from the family that owned that plantation back there, the other side of the city. Tell me more 'bout that, it sounds interestin'."

"Her family owned a lot of the land we're on now, too." John stood and stretched his arms while yawning. "The funny thing is, my grandfather owned a lot of this land too."

"Shit." Billy spread out the syllables. "I can't believe a poor man like you ever came from someone who owned this much land."

"After he died, his wife and son sold all of it off to pay debts and live off of, none of it has been in my family for a long time; the land's all gone, and so is the money, it's all gone." John sat back down next to the fire. "Janice's family had a great deal of land holdings around here, and back where we all live."

"She mustta come from a rich family," Billy said. "So, why ain't y'all rich now?"

"Her family had a pile of money a hundred fifty years ago, but both her parents worked as school teachers in New England, and believe me, they are far from rich."

"So?" Tim asked. "What happened?"

"The same thing that happened to almost the entire planter class in the old South, they lost it all in the war, and those who didn't bank enough money in England, or somewhere else safe, became a new class of aristocratic poor," John replied.

146

"They built their fortunes under a system which was doomed, and some of them had to leave the South. Janice's ancestors moved North and used their education to make a living; her great grandfather was a doctor, and he married a Yankee."

"Who kept the family's old plantation then?" Al asked. "I thought it stayed in that family until recently?"

"After the Civil War some long lost cousin took possession of it."

"How long did he keep it?" Tim asked

"That son of a bitch lynched a lot of folks who had taken up farming on the old plantation land. They scared away the rest.," John sighed.

"Oh," Al said. "Did he pay anything for the land when he took it?"

"What do you think?" John sounded disgusted.

"Didn't the blood relatives get anything when he took back all the land?" Tim asked.

"After the war, the new land barons had a mean streak in them, they became the aristocracy then, who wouldn't share the power with anyone."

"So?" Billy asked. "Why should they, they fought for it, 'n they won it; I say more power to 'em."

John rubbed his eyes as he stared into the sooty flames, "I say what I said before, this land belongs to no one. We all share it, and we're all a part of it but no one can take what isn't theirs."

"Whatever," Billy said in a disgusted tone of voice, then fell silent.

Tim asked, "What about your family's land, were they rich plantation owners?"

John replied, "No, my great grandfather was a Yankee who paid cash for land in the late eighteen hundreds. From what my father told me, his family didn't have much cash after the old man died, so they had to sell it all."

"It was kind of an investment?" Al asked.

"Sort of an investment," John agreed quietly.

147

Al walked to the dwindling wood pile next to the tent and picked up an armful of wood then brought it to the side of the camp fire. He added a few more pieces to the flames before sitting back down. They all were silent for an hour, each man was company to only his own thoughts while they all looked at the flames dancing and spitting in the dark of the cold Fall night.

As the fire slowly faded, John spoke, "Do you ever notice how the forest looks like it closes in on you when the fire dies down?"

The others looked at him, not speaking.

"I mean, when the moon hasn't risen yet, like tonight, the tall trees materialize into a dark wall. You can't make them out individually." John tried to clarify his point. "The branches give the impression of growing together to increase the darkness." .

"And the bogy man comes out 'n eats you up, right?" Billy grinned at John, then at the others.

"I'm not afraid of anything, I think it's kind of beautiful," John replied. "Like the sounds of the forest are different at night, the visual impression is also different, but just as beautiful."

"Yeah," Tim interrupted. "I always thought the woods were real nice after dark, the animals appear to be happier."

"How 'n the hell can you tell a happy animal from a sad one in the dark?" Billy laughed.

"By the way they sound," Tim answered, glancing sideways at Billy. "They sound happier to me, I like the night in the woods, if it only weren't so cold."

"Amen to that," Al said loudly. "I'm goin' into the tent 'n try my best to stay warm."

It was fifteen minutes past nine when they all climbed into the tent for another cold night.

148

Chapter 14

We think our fathers fools, so wise we grow;
Our wiser sons, no doubt will think us so.

Alexander Pope, Essay on Criticism.

A tall lanky man rode a mottled brown horse at a slow trot, raising a small cloud of dust on the narrow dirt path leading from the river crossing to the Rose Community. To keep the dust from his clothes underneath, the rider wore a long riding coat, but the heat of the early Summer morning made him open the collar wide.

In his late thirties, with dark black hair, dark eyes and a square set jaw, the man slowly dismounted in front of Abraham Rose's house. Tying his horse to a small pine tree, he took off the dust jacket, carefully placed it over the saddle of his horse, brushed off his expensively tailored suit then walked to the front door.

Abraham Rose, standing in his living room, looked out the front window at the approaching stranger.

"Hello, my name is Ralph Barrington," The stranger said.

Abraham opened the front door to his house wider and smiled as Ralph paused at the door, standing a head taller than Abraham.

"Welcome to our home, sir, my name is Abraham Rose, and these are my children." Abraham waved his hand towards several young men and boys seated at the wooden table in the living room; he signaled for one of them to locate their missing friend.

149

"My wife is visiting at the moment with some of our daughters, but please do stay and meet her and the rest of my family," Abraham said.

"Thank you, I was planning to stay only briefly, but I would be pleased to meet your wife, will she be long?"

"No." Abraham motioned Ralph to an upholstered chair against the front wall of the living room. "Please be seated and we'll talk while we wait."

"I shall."

Abraham turned to the gathering of boys at the table. "Sam, go and see to this man's horse."

The wooden home was simply decorated. The dining room and living room shared the same large expanse, a large wooden table with many handmade chairs grouped around it occupied a space in the dining area. Several family tintypes hung on the living room wall; beneath them an upholstered chair and sofa, along with two other hand made wooden chairs resided in the living room for guests to use. Three doors led off from the dining room and living room; two of these doors led to bedrooms, the other led eventually to a kitchen attached to the back of the house. Narrow wooden stairs to the far left of the living room led up to two more bedrooms squeezed into what should have been an attic. One large rug lay on the living room floor. The home was spotless.

"Thank you." Ralph sat down. "I'm on my way to Texas."

Abraham looked at the boys seated at the table and stroked his bristly beard. "Please go get your brothers."

All the boys left quickly through the front door.

"This seems a bit out of your way," Abraham observed.

"I know it does, but I had some unfinished business in the area, and this was recommended as a fine place to visit on my way to the main road west."

"So, you have completed your business here?" Abraham watched his visitor carefully.

150

"Yes I have, the person I was looking for died many years ago, but other than that, the trip through this state has been profitable."

"What line of business are you in?"

"I buy and sell land for investors up North," Ralph paused, considering how much to tell this stranger. "My father and my brother own several factories in New England and they always want me to join them in the family business, but I like the travel and freedom this job gives me. I travel and others pay my expenses, all my investors are wealthy men who let me spend their money, and I enjoy that part of it very much."

"I can see that, sir." Abraham looked intensely into Ralph's eyes. "But I have the feeling that you have come to this place to find someone."

"I have," Ralph answered quickly. "I met a woman during the war, and I needed to see her again to conclude some unfinished things between us."

"Did you find her?" Abraham's dark brown eyes sparkled.

"I found her grave."

"Did you finish your business with her?"

"If she heard me, I did."

Abraham relaxed and stepped a few paces towards the table before he spoke, "I'm sure she did, I know she heard you. What, then, brings you here?"

"Strange as it sounds, another grave brought me here."

"Could you explain that?"

"The woman I came to talk to, when I knew her during the war; had a servant. This servant could also have helped me, but she too has died." Ralph took in a deep breath and focused his eyes through a far window. "The tenants near the small grave yard told me that this servant had a son, I believe they told me his name was Paul."

"Paul is here, he's at the mill right now loading grain. I have sent my sons for him, and he will be here before supper. Will you join us for supper?"

151

Ralph relaxed, then returned his attention to Abraham. "I shall, if you feel I should."

"The Lord has sent you here, here you must be."

"I cannot stay for long, my clients expect me back in a little over one year, and I still have Alabama, Mississippi, Louisiana, and the whole state of Texas to go through."

Abraham reached for a straight backed wooden chair, pulled under the rough wooden dining room table; he placed it facing Ralph, then he sat down. Ralph's attention once again went through the distant window. He felt comfortable, at home as he watched a small group of young children play with two barrel hoops in an open area. The air, thick with humidity, washed over everything like waves over a beach. The tall trees which surrounded the house and yard slowly twisted their leaves in the hot afternoon breeze. Evening crow calls, Summer insects, and children laughing filled the short silence between the two men.

"It is quite peaceful here, a person could do a lot worse than to spend the rest of his life at this place." Ralph continued to look through the window.

"Peace comes from within, not the surroundings." Abraham cleared his throat. "Do you go about buying land, only to spend money for these people?"

"No." Ralph replied. "They have maps of the areas they want, and I try to buy as much of it as I can, for as little money as I can. They also list the most money they are willing to pay for each tract of land."

"Why do these few men want so much land?"

"Some of them want it for rail lines, others want to build textile factories closer to the crops, and still others want to control the supply of cotton to their factories up North," Ralph paused. "Land is cheap in the south these days."

Abraham leaned forward in his chair. "God's land is not cheap, men cheapen it."

Ralph shifted in his chair. "Land is business." He paused in Abraham's silence. "This whole area is beautiful, the virgin

152

forest remains in some parts, it's a different story from much of the land surrounding you."

"We only cut small areas for people to grow what we need to eat, nothing more. We need little to live in God's world besides our faith, and we take only what we must from His land."

"Who owns all this?" Ralph again shifted in his chair.

"Are the investors interested in our land?"

Ralph shook his head slowly. "No, not your place, I was curious."

"My two brothers and I hold title to this land," Abraham said. "But we all use it to live on, equally. It is safer if a white person holds title to land in this place and time, but that too may change I pray."

That's why I fought the war." Ralph sat up straight in his chair. "Niggers have as much right as any to own the land they work."

"Please do not use 'nigger' in front of Paul. Although he is your son and as white as you are, he still thinks himself a negro like the fine people who raised him."

"Sir." Ralph verbally stumbled as he opened his eyes wide and leaned back defensively. "I do not have a son, I am unmarried."

"I do not judge any man's actions, only God shall judge man, and He has sent you here."

Ralph fell silent for a full minute, his eyes looked out the window, and his senses were again filled with the sounds of the forest and of the children playing.

"Does he know?" Ralph quietly sank back into his seat.

"Paul knows only that his real mother was Sarah Appleby, the white woman who owned the land he was born on and who owned the only parents he knew and loved as his own."

Ralph spoke after a brief pause, "May I stay here for a while with you?"

Abraham grinned almost to a laugh, "I told you that God sent you here, and you are welcome here as long as God wants you to stay."

153

....

"You say you ain't got any catfish like these up North, Mr. Barrington."

Paul idly bobbed his fishing pole up and down over the muddy brown river, the line dripped water on each upstroke.

"Not quite like these," Ralph said. "They're real good tasting, aren't they?"

"I always like them." Paul looked into the moving water. "My daddy, John, taught me the best way to clean them."

"It is easy that way, but I haven't yet got the hang of it." Ralph looked down river at the mill, the midday sun glared off the whitewashed wall facing them.

"You're my real daddy, ain't you?" Paul abruptly asked.

"Did Abraham tell you?" Ralph looked at Paul without letting his emotions show.

"Naw, he didn't tell me anything, I saw my birth record and I know I was born in time for some Yankee to have gotten with my real mama." Paul turned a slight shade of pink and cleared his throat. "Well, you know what I mean, she had me right when the war ended. And, you and I got the same color hair and eyes."

"I know what you mean, and yes, I am your real father as best as I can figure," Ralph answered.

"Well." Paul nervously looked back down at the river. "What do we do now?"

"What do you want to do?"

Ralph's question escaped unanswered into the late morning air as the two of them stood in silence for a few minutes.

"The Rose's have treated you well since you've come to live with them," Ralph broke the silence.

"They sure have."

"Do you want to stay here?"

"I don't know any more; I'm sixteen now, and I don't know." Paul considered his answer carefully, his face wrinkling in thought. "I like the people here, but I've seen too many bad

154

things these past few years. Most of the people I know like me have been killed by white folks like you." He moved his gaze back to the river. "And I don't like the place, but I love the people right here where I live, do you understand what I'm sayin'?"

"What do you feel like doing?"

"I feel like getting to know you a little better, you ain't so bad, and you are my real daddy." Paul looked at Ralph. "I loved my first daddy, John, a whole lot, but he ain't been here for a lotta years. Mr. Rose is real nice, so is his wife, they have taught me so much while I've been here. Mrs. Rose taught me to read and write, and how to talk like the rich folks."

"What about Mary?"

"I don't want to think about her any more, she wasn't any mother to me, but Mr. Rose says I should love her anyway because she tried as best she could."

"I think she did," Ralph paused. "Do you remember Miss Sarah Bellows at all?"

"You mean Mrs. Appleby?"

"Yes."

"I don't remember her at all; I do remember her land, and how Mary and daddy would always fight over that little place she gave to them for me."

"Yes, Abraham told me how Mr. Appleby stole that land from you, and how you still have the deed to it."

"Ain't gonna do no good," Paul replied with a frown. "White men own it now, and no colored's ever going to change that."

Ralph didn't know exactly how to handle his son's feelings, but he plunged ahead anyway with what he thought might help the situation,

"My son's not a nigger and anyway I don't think that has to be the way it is."

"I wish you wouldn't use that word," Paul said softly.

"What word?" Ralph asked.

155

"The night those man hanged the daddy that raised me and the day they beat the mama that loved me, they called them niggers, and they called me one too. Puts a knot in my stomach like I ain't a man and I'm gonna die." Paul looked at the ground. "I know what you're sayin', but that's what I feel."

"I fought a war to free slaves like the folks who raised you," Ralph sounded confused as he rubbed the side of his face.

"I know." Paul looked directly at his father. "Those folks who raised me were fighting that war before you came here, and they'll fight it long after both of us are gone."

"I won't call them that any more," Ralph said, to acknowledge his son's view. "Did you hear what I said before?"

"You acted like you knew something about the Appleby land."

"I know that Appleby doesn't own that land anymore, he sold it to pay off all the debts he's run up."

"You mean it?" Paul dropped his fishing pole on the bank, looking directly into Ralph's face.

"The sorry son of a bitch sold me a three thousand acre tract."

"To you?"

"To me and I would be happy to honor your deed to the fifty acres, and throw in a few hundred more, if you want to go back there."

"I don't want to see those lily white bastard crackers any more unless I see them dead."

"But, Paul," Ralph said, agitated at his son's continued insistence of his racial makeup. "As I told you, both your mother and I are pure white, you have not one speck of dark blood in you so why would you object to living with your own kind?"

"I know I'm white, but I ain't their kind of white, besides those bastards treat me like they treated the people who raised me. One thing I've learned in the past few years is that there's white folks, and then there's those white folks, and I ain't never going to live with those bastard lily white crackers. You ought to know them, you're white and you fought 'em in the war; they ain't

156

like the Roses, not at all. They can take their precious land and kiss it, all I want to do with it is to bury them on it."

"So, what are you going to do?" Ralph slowly looked down the river, not fully understanding his son's motivation. He could appreciate Paul's anger at the men who murdered his adopted father, but he couldn't fathom the disgust Paul generalized towards the whole white race, to which he himself belonged.

"Don't know exactly what I want to do," Paul replied.

"Do you want some more time to think about it? I shall be back through here in about a year."

"Don't need that much time; my love for the Rose folks ain't as much as the hate for the rest of the white folks and the land they own. They still think they're better than us and they think they still own the free coloreds like they own the land, but they don't own neither."

"Don't forget, I'm one of those white folks." Ralph sounded nervous.

"No you ain't, you're a Yankee, and they think you're like me. The only reason they treat you well is because you have a lot of money to spend."

"Ha," Ralph laughed out loud. "Then you and I can be friends, eh?"

"Don't see why not." Paul looked at Ralph and grinned. "A son should get along with his father."

"So, what do you feel like doing?" Ralph asked again.

"I want to go with you for a while, I want to learn what the rest of this country's like." Paul picked back up his fishing pole. "I don't want to live on this land anymore, it means nothing to me, I never put no roots in it anyway. Where are we going?"

Ralph laughed out loud, "Texas, son, Texas."

157

Chapter 15

Death destroys a man: the idea of Death saves him.
E. M. Forster, Howards End

J ohn was the first to open his eyes; he poked his head near the closed front tent flap, noting that the sunlight was not as bright as it had been the day before. Wispy clouds raced high above almost leafless trees, though thin, clouds covered the whole section of the sky that he could see. Small flocks of birds darted about in the gray sky, while a lone hawk rode on an updraft, moving his wings slightly as he changed direction, looking for his morning meal.

Tim stirred in his sleeping bag, but did not awaken as John looked at his watch; it was twenty minutes to nine. In the gray light, the sun was forty five minutes above the horizon, not as early as he had thought.

"What time is it?" Al groggily sat up.

Tim opened his eyes and looked at John.

"It's twenty minutes before nine," John answered.

"Damn, we missed dawn again," Tim said in a slightly annoyed tone.

"I have a feeling more than one thing hasn't dawned on us yet," John whispered to himself.

"Looks damned dark out there," Billy said, still laying down. "You sure it's that late?"

"That's what my watch says." John assured him.

John looked to the back of the tent where Billy was sprawled inside his sleeping bag.

"We'd better get up," John added

"Maybe your watch is wrong." Billy rubbed his eyes.

John shrugged, "I don't think so."

"Could'a run down." Billy rose on his elbows.

"It's a self winding Omega Seamaster," John insisted. "It doesn't run down as long as I wear it."

"Don't get your panties in a wad." Billy fell back down into his sleeping bag. "Just remember you got that thing at a pawn shop."

"My watch is a quartz, and the battery's fine," Al interjected. "I got the same time as John's watch."

"It's cold as hell in here," Tim said, to change the subject. "I hope it's not colder out there."

"You know it is," Al sighed. "I'll bet we get snow today," he paused to let his breath out all the way, then take in another deep one. "That's all we need, more snow and more cold, wet traveling."

"Why don't we stay here, start our fire again, 'n wait for someone to come to us?" Billy asked, sitting up.

Al looked thoughtfully towards Billy. "That maybe don't sound too dumb after all."

"The river's got to be real close by," Tim said. "I don't see why we don't make it to the river, then we'll be home free."

"I agree with Tim." John confidently looked at each of the other men, one at a time. "We ought to get to the river, then go up stream for help."

"Why don't we compromise then?" Al asked. "We'll stay here 'till noon with the fire goin', then we'll take off for the river if we don't see nobody."

The other three looked at each other in silence, thinking.

"It's okay with me," Tim said. "I'd like to take it easy today anyway, least ways easier than we did yesterday."

"Okay," John added. "We've got plenty of food, and we're not too far from the river, and the bridge," he paused. "So I guess it couldn't hurt to stay here for a while, not until noon, but late morning at least."

"Good deal." Billy pulled himself from his sleeping bag and stuck his feet into his boots.

159

The other three men followed suit, carefully dressing with extra layers as they plunged outside into the cold, gray air. After going through morning rituals, they wandered around the camp site collecting wood for the morning fire.

Al collected as many pine needles as he could hold in both his hands before returning to the remains of the previous night's fire. Sifting ashes, he uncovered several glowing coals, and coaxed the smoldering pine needles he lay on them into flames. Adding wood, he worked the flames into a large enough fire for the four men to huddle around.

Tim had suspended all the uneaten cooked venison from a tall branch the night before. After reheating it over the fire, they all began to eat strips of warm, cooked meat.

"This meat ain't no better than last night." Billy continued chewing. "Fire cookin' makes this stuff like shoe leather."

"You're right," John agreed. "But, it's better than cold beans."

"I'm sure glad we ain't gettin' out too soon today." Tim cut a bite-sized hunk of deer meat off a larger strip.

"Why's that?" Al asked. "We ain't got up too early for the last two days, ya know."

"I don't mind getting up late," John said. "I feel better with the extra sleep."

"What's the point of getting up early anyway," Billy broke in. "We ain't goin' huntin' no way."

"But we are trying to hunt our way out of here," John contradicted him.

"I have a good feeling about today." Al nodded his head and cleared his throat. "We're going to get out of this place today."

"What makes you think that?" Billy asked.

"I don't know, it's a feeling, that's all."

"I hope you're right, Al," Tim said. "It's about time we got somewhere familiar."

160

"Hell," Al proclaimed. "I'm having a better time this year than I did the last ten times out."

"But we're lost and might be here for weeks." Tim protested.

"And, don't forget, we might also be a million years in the past," Billy said, and laughed.

Tim looked at John. "I've been thinking."

"That could be dangerous," Billy teased.

"At least he thinks." John looked at Billy.

"Well," Tim continued. "We could be in the future as well as in the past." he paused while the others digested this thought. "You said that the forest is timeless and we could be lost in that timelessness."

"That's possible," John replied. "I suppose, if we're lost in time, we could be anywhere, in the future or the past."

"Well," Tim continued. "We can't tell anything from these woods, so the only way we'll find out when we're at is to see another person, not talk to them like Billy did yesterday, but actually see them."

"A frame of reference," John said.

"Will you two cut the crap out," Al insisted. "We're in the National Forest, and we're less than a mile to the river," Al paused. "And that's that."

"You're a pill, Al." Billy stood up and stretched. "Even I believe this time crap, how else can I explain all this strange junk out here?"

"I keep hearin' that," Al said. "But, I still don't buy it."

"I didn't mean to start anything by what I said a few days ago," John interrupted. "Let's forget what I said about the time stuff, okay?"

"Not okay," Tim sounded annoyed. "I think it's an interesting explanation of all this, and I'm not through following it."

"It's not logical," Al insisted. "Time goes from here to there, and we're followin' it like a hound dog follows a track,

161

there ain't no way that hound dog could be in two places at the same time."

"What a great scientist," Billy laughed. "You got another animal theory to explain the meaning of life?" Billy chuckled.

"All I heard you come up with is - Yep, I'll believe anything you say," Al taunted.

"Watch what you say." Billy jammed his index finger towards Al.

"Come on," Tim interrupted. "He's got a right to his opinion."

"Forget what I said," John insisted. "We need to work together to get out of here, not fight about what time it is."

Al laughed out loud, "That's the first time you've made a damned bit of sense."

"Well, I don't give a flip what any of you say, I'm gonna mark where we hit the river with my extra orange vest, 'n I'm comin' back here 'n look for all these trees which ain't supposed to be here, 'n all these animals which can't be here," Billy insisted.

"That's all right by me, but why don't you help me tear the tent down first." Tim walked to the tent, disappearing into it then tossing out everybody's gear.

Al and John stuffed everything into their packs, and placed their rifles on top of them. John pulled Tim's pack near the dying flames of their morning fire, and stowed his gear in it for him; Al did the same with Billy's backpack.

Billy stood still, holding a tent pole, and motioning the others with his free hand to keep quiet.

"What is it?" Al whispered.

"You hear the footsteps?" Tim asked quietly.

"Listen to the squirrels pitchin' a fit," Al whispered loudly. "I don't hear nothin' else."

"I do, now," John said in a whisper, walking closer to the others. "It might be the people who've been camping near us for the last two nights, it could even be that Mark kid Billy heard."

162

"It also might be that bear I ran into a few days ago." Billy walked towards his rifle.

"I can't see nothin'." Al crouched to see through the thick forest of branches and bushes ahead of him.

"No noise, now," John said quietly. "The animals know what's out there." He stretched his silence to match the forest's. "I think I know what's out there too."

Billy reached inside his pack and pulled out a small handful of cartridges; he stuffed them, one by one, into the magazine of his seven millimeter magnum.

"Be careful, Billy," Al whispered to Billy. "We don't know what's there, it could be another hunter."

"Also could be that damn bear." Billy closed the bolt on his rifle and clicked the safety on.

Far away in the distant tree line, a dark form appeared, walking slowly. John took three steps to his right to get a better vantage point, then gave a start, a slight expression of recognition. He moved swiftly towards his rifle and pack which lay on the ground ahead of him. As his left foot hit the ground on his second step, a twig broke under it.

A thundering boom echoed from the area in front of them. John felt himself shoved back slightly, he spun a quarter turn to his left and lost his balance, dropping to the ground. A sharp, burning sensation in his left side made him crumple his arms to his stomach.

Staring in the direction of the blast, Tim, Al, and Billy did not see their friend fall. They watched the form of a man step from behind a tree, about one hundred yards ahead of them, He pointed a rifle at them; several trees over, another man held a smoking rifle. Lowering his rifle, the shooter took a side step away from the tree trunk. Even one hundred yards away, his form stood out clearly in the distant gray and brown forest. At that instant John hit the ground and Billy looked sharply around. Blood oozed from John's side between the fingers of his right hand pressed against the his abdomen, blood stained the brown leaves on the ground beneath him.

163

Billy shouted, "Hit the dirt!"

The figure who had fired shouted, "Die, you bastards, die."

Al bellowed, "Hold your fire, hold your fire, you're shooting at people."

"'Course we're shootin' at you," a strong voice from the woods echoed. "We're at war, are you stupid or sumpthin'?"

Dropping like a stone, Billy swung his rifle to his shoulder as soon as he hit the ground. Pressing the rifle stock firmly against his cheek, he began to track the shapes silhouetted against the forest ahead.

Al dove towards his rifle as he headed to the ground, while Tim dropped to the ground and began wriggling towards John.

"Kill them sons of bitches." Tim crawled to John. "They shot John."

Billy fired one round after another until his magazine was empty. One of the men in the woods ahead of them fell backwards, his rifle firing as it pointed to the sky; a flash of fire exploded next to two other trees ahead of them. There followed a loud thud on a tree next to Al, and a whizzing sound near their half torn down tent.

Al reached his rifle and began loading it. Pausing, he reached for Billy's back pack and threw it to him.

Al fired two shots in the direction of one of the flashes; a loud groan echoed as the sound of Al's last shot quieted.

Billy reloaded his rifle and looked through the scope, not firing at anything.

"There's five or six of 'em." Billy strained his eyes to look harder through his scope. "I think we got two more 'n they're pullin' the wounded back into the forest."

"What the hell's goin' on?" Al pulled his rifle stock back up to his cheek and peered through his scope.

"Hell." Al pulled his rifle back off his cheek and laid it down on the ground beside him.

164

"I saw it too." Billy looked in Al's direction. "What the hell do ya say now?"

"Shit." Al let out a full breath as he looked back in the direction of the men who had fired on them. "It can't be, it's got to be a joke or somethin'."

Tim sat up and shouted to Al and Billy. "This ain't no joke, John's been shot and he's bleedin' real bad."

"Oh, God." Al crawled to John and Tim as quickly as he could, staying in a squatting position while carrying his rifle cradled in his arms.

"I'm stayin' here, lookin' for those sons of bitches." Billy remained where he was, looking intensely out into the forest. "You need anythin'?"

"Throw me my pack," Al shouted.

Never letting his eyes leave the direction of the distant men, Billy scooted to Al's pack, then threw it as far as he could in John's direction. Tim dragged the pack to Al, who was cautiously removing John's coat and even more carefully unbuttoning his shirt.

"I've got a first aid kit in the side pocket," Al said, not looking up from John's wound.

"What the hell happened, why did they shoot us?" John asked quietly.

"I don't know." Al tried to reassure him. "But they only nicked you, the rest of us are all right."

"Nicked me?" John asked, in a faint voice. "I'll be lucky if I don't lose a kidney; look at where the hole is."

"I see it," Tim said with a grim expression on his face. "How do you feel?"

"I feel like I'll live, but it hurts like hell right now."

"Do you feel cold?" Al asked.

"No, I don't think I'm in shock, but don't leave me uncovered for too long."

Al looked at Tim for a second before he spoke, "We've got to stop the bleeding right now."

"Is it coming out of both sides?" Tim asked.

165

Al gently lifted John, checking for damage in his back.

"Yeah," Al said. "We got to stop the blood."

"How?" Tim asked.

"Burn it shut," John grunted as the pain became more acute.

"What?" Tim asked.

"You heard me," John's voice was labored. "If the bleeding isn't stopped, I'll bleed to death."

"Sealing the outer holes won't stop any internal bleeding," Al grimly said.

"I know," John grimaced. "We can't do anything about that now, but we have to stop the bleeding we can see for now."

"Go put this knife blade into the coals on the fire over there." Al handed Tim a long blade hunting knife from a scabbard underneath his jacket. "Leave it there 'till it gets hot; I'll drag John to it, wait there for us."

"How's he doin'?" Billy shouted.

"Fine." Al pulled an undershirt from his pack and tore it in half. "You keep those bastards from comin' too close."

"You got it."

Al pocketed his forty four and pulled off his leather belt. He put half of the undershirt on the back side of John's wound, and the other half on the front. He then strapped the belt around John, securing both bandages. Carefully slipping John's coat back on, Al began to slowly pull him towards the fire and Tim.

Billy lowered himself from his sitting position to a prone position and brought his rifle into firing position; he took a careful aim into the brown tangle of woods, and fired.

"Ha, mine'll go one hell of a lot further than yours, you fuckers," Billy chuckled.

"What happened?" Al called to Billy as he arrived at the fire with John.

"I got another one," Billy laughed nervously. "They was standin' there, lookin' at us through a spy glass, like they was safe

166

or somethin'." He looked through his scope again. "I blew his ass off, 'n they's movin' farther back."

"How far are they?" Al asked.

"'Bout five, or six hundred yards by now, can't see a damned thing any more, they disappeared into the woods." Billy looked back through his scope. "I guessed on the drop, 'n I got 'em at 'bout four hundred yards, y'all should've seen 'em run."

"The range of their rifles ain't that far." Al lay John next to the fire and slipped his coat back off. "They don't know how far our rifles'll go."

"What are you talkin' about?" Tim asked.

"What we saw through our scopes," Al replied.

"What did you see?" John groaned.

"Young men dressed like they used to a hundred fifty years ago, a few of them was in old rebel uniforms, least ways they was wearin' the caps; they was all shootin' at us with muskets," Al said flatly.

"What?" Tim asked.

"Well." John made a contorted expression, with his eyes clenched shut. "We now know when we are, don't we?"

"It's hot, Al," Tim interrupted.

"Do it." John opened his eyes and stared into Al's face.

Al silently slipped off John's shirt and removed a glove from his coat pocket. Dripping Betadine from a small bottle into the wound, Al then blew on it to air dry it as much as possible. Al lifted up the hot knife with his gloved hand. He placed the hot knife onto the back wound; a small puff of rancid smelling smoke rose from the wound. John shouted with a full breath of air as the knife melted and seared his flesh.

Al let go of the breath he had been holding, then placed the knife back in the coals of the fire.

"In a minute, I'll do the front," Al sounded quite somber.

"Ain't nothin' in there, right?" Tim asked.

"No, it's a clean shot through and through, I hope he don't bleed inside too bad," Al paused. "There ain't too much

167

none of us can do for that. All we can do is try to prevent infection from startin' up."

Al grabbed the knife again and sealed the entry wound as he had done with the exit wound; John screamed again, falling unconscious this time.

Tim pulled an undershirt from his pack and made new bandages, soaked with antiseptic. He tied the bandages to John with Al's belt, then re-buttoned John's shirt, and his coat. Al retrieved his rifle, loading it with as many cartridges as it would hold. Tim lay John's head on a pair of pants from his back pack, then he retrieved John's rifle and loaded it.

"You sure we should've done that?" Tim asked.

"Yeah," Al sounded as sure as anyone could. "John asked for it, he knew we have to travel soon and that no bandage would've kept him from bleedin' to death, this was the only way."

"What now?" Tim asked.

"We get the hell outta here fast," Billy loudly whispered. "Before they come back, we get lost in the woods."

"First we get rid of these orange vests we got on," Al added.

They all pulled off their hunter's orange vests and threw them onto the ground. Billy rose to a crouching posture and moved to the others while Tim raised his rifle and looked through the scope in the direction the other men had disappeared.

"Where'd they all go?" Tim asked.

"Out there." Billy pointed in the general direction of south west. "What do we do 'bout John?"

"We take him with us," Al insisted.

"Yeah, but how?"

"We make some sort of a carrying cart, or somethin'," Al answered.

"How?" Billy asked.

"You tell me; don't be such a pain in the ass," Al complained.

168

"I'll tell you," Billy replied. "You remember all those cowboy movies?"

"So?" Al shrugged his shoulders.

"So, we make a sling with two long poles 'n the tent, like the Indians did in the movies; we put John in it, 'n we take turns pullin' him."

"We can't pull somethin' that big through all this heavy brush," Tim said.

"If we make it only wide enough to carry John, we can," Billy sounded proud of his contribution. "Make it in a V shape with the small end draggin' on the ground."

"That might work," Al agreed.

"See, I ain't so dumb," Billy said.

"Let's get on with it, you two." Tim started to climb down to them.

"No," Billy said. "You stay up there, 'n keep an eye out for those guys. Watch all directions, they might decide to circle back on us."

"Okay." Tim turned around. He looked through his scope, then lowered the rifle to study the nest of brambles and trees before him. As he watched for movement, a shadow or branch would catch his attention briefly, then he would pick up where he left off, scanning the horizon.

169

Chapter 16

To fear the worst oft cures the worse.

William Shakespeare Troilus and Cressida, act 3, sc. 2

John opened his eyes, it was daytime. The sky was still gray and the temperature hovered below freezing as a light breeze ever so gently pushed the tallest trees from the south-west. Tim was next to him, looking intently into the forest.

"What's going on?" John spoke in a labored voice.

Tim quickly turned his head to face John, then turned to his left.

"He's come to," Tim announced.

"Great." Al walked to John's side. "We've got it built."

"What?" John ask, dazed, squinting as he looked up at Al.

"Your chariot," Al replied, pointing to the sling he and Billy had finished.

John lifted himself and turned his head to look, grunted, then fell back on the ground.

"Save your strength." Billy laid John's rifle on top of him. "Keep your rifle handy, they may come back."

"Is it loaded?" John asked.

"Yeah, I put a full clip in it."

"Which clip?" John asked.

"The full clip," Billy replied. "We saw the two round clip, but we found the bunch of eight round ones in your pack."

"Thanks," John whispered.

170

He opened the action of his rifle and removed one round from the clip, then let the bolt down on the empty chamber.

"I don't want to shoot my toe off on top of the hole in my belly." He added.

"Suit yourself," Billy said, walking to the sling. He and Al carefully lifted John, then set him back down in the sling.

"We put a stick down at the bottom for you to hook your boots on." Al placed one of John's boots on it. "That'll keep you from slippin' off when we drag you."

John silently did as he was told.

"Come on." Billy nervously grabbed John's back pack and laid it across the sling, above his head. "Let's get the hell outta here."

Billy lay John's rifle next to him in the sling, "I hope you can shoot this thing fast if need be."

"Fast enough," John replied.

The four men walked along the edge of the swamp in a tight line. They moved noisily, but at a quick pace. Billy pulled John on the sling made from the tent fabric folded over several times and stretched between two long poles made from sapling pine trunks while Tim followed behind, looking periodically over his shoulder. Al and Tim looked so intensely into the forest around them, that they occasionally tripped on an unseen branch, or a tangle of vines.

At the end of the first half mile of their march, Al motioned for the group to stop.

"What's wrong?" Tim was breathing so hard, he was almost panting.

"Let's listen for other footsteps." Al caught his breath. "Listen for 'em."

The four men were silent; the syncopated sounds of four breaths evening out as one, alone and afraid, filled the silence.

"Where's all the animals? I can't see anything moving out there at all, where is everything?" John asked, lifting himself for a moment. He fell back.

"Put yourself in their place," Tim answered. "What would you do if you saw this parade crashing through your forest?"

"I see what you mean," John laughed faintly.

"Whatever," Billy sighed. "I don't hear nothin' followin' us, so let's get goin'."

They trotted for another three quarters of a mile through the thick brush of the swamp, constantly changing directions to avoid the cold thick mud.

They did not speak, except for the times John fell out of his sling.

"Goddamn it." John hit the snow frosted ground. "This ground's frozen, and my side feels like it's on fire."

"Put him back on," Billy barked to Tim.

"Yes, sir." Tim lifted John gently back on the sling.

"Give me your belt," Al growled at Billy.

"What?" Billy asked, still holding the two poles of the sling in his hands.

"I said put that thing down, and give me your belt," Al repeated.

"Why?"

"I'm goin' to tie mine 'n yours together, 'n strap him in there."

"Oh." Billy complied. "How do I keep my pants from fallin' down?"

"Look at what I did." Al pointed to his waist. "Pull your shirt out and tie it through your belt loops in a few places, its kind of like suspenders."

Tim strapped the two belts around the sling and John, below his armpits. Tim walked to the front of the sling, and lifted it.

"I'll pull him for a while, you take up the rear," Tim said.

It was two in the afternoon when Al stopped the group before they entered the first clearing they had encountered that day.

"What's up there?" Billy asked.

172

"Don't know." Al scanned the area ahead of them. "Might be a farm, or might be a meadow."

"I'll stay with John." Tim lowered the sling. "You two go on ahead slowly 'n let me know if I should follow."

"Right." Al moved his rifle to the two hand carry and walked slowly to the clearing; Billy followed him, moving up to Al's right.

Tim watched as they moved through the trees and into the clearing. In a second, Al reappeared and motioned Tim to follow. Tim lifted the sling with John in it back up and trotted towards Al.

Ahead of them was a dirt road, with little sign of recent travel. Fifty yards beyond the road was the river, the brown water quietly moving within its banks. The road was narrow with dried brown grasses growing from all parts of it. Deep narrow ruts wandered along the road, white snow filled some, ice filled others.

"What you make of this?" Billy asked the others. "I don't remember no road next to the river, the only dirt road into the forest is the one we came in on, 'n that weren't near the river. like everythin' else on this trip, this ain't what it's supposed to be."

"Look," Al spoke to John in his sling. "I don't know what's goin' on, but we have to go with what we really see, not what we think we see."

"What does that mean?" Tim asked.

"That means we go up river now," Al insisted. "No matter when or where we are, this river has always flowed away from the bigger town, so if we go up river, we'll get to someone sooner or later."

"But, Greensboro is only ten miles down river," Billy interrupted "We might ought to go that way."

"That ain't a big enough town," Al objected. "Besides, more people live up river than down, so our chance of findin' somebody is greater that way."

"What do you think?" Tim asked John.

173

"Go up the road," John replied weakly. "It's the only option facing us."

"I ain't in the mood to argue." Billy shouldered his rifle. "Al, you drag John for a while."

"Where do we camp tonight?" Al lifted John and began walking up the road with Tim falling in line after him.

"Between the road 'n the river, we'd have a better view of who's commin', 'n no one can get behind us," Tim answered.

"Good idea." Billy took the lead. "Let's get as much distance as we can behind us before dark."

They walked, slower than before, until the sun fell low in the Western sky, still partially masked by thickening gray skies.

"What time you got?" Billy asked.

Al pulled back his coat sleeve to check the time of day, "Four thirty."

"How 'bout that spot over there?" Tim pointed to a small clearing through a thick growth of brush.

"Let's stop." Al agreed.

Al surveyed the spot and moved towards it with John dragging behind while Billy moved some of the brush out of Al's way as he dragged John into the clearing.

"This'll be a damn good spot." Billy looked around the small clearing. "We can see anyone comin' from either direction on the road, 'n they can't see us at all."

"Yeah, 'n there's this stand of bushes between us 'n the river." Tim added. "It's about as safe as we can expect from all sides."

"What about the tent?" John asked from his sling.

"You must be gettin' better to ask 'bout that," Al observed.

"I guess," John responded.

"We thought 'bout that while you was out cold," Al said. "We left the tent poles back at the other camp so we 're gonna undo your sling, 'n use the fabric 'n rope to make a tent between two trees."

"Did you bring the tent stakes?" John asked.

174

"We ain't stupid," Billy replied.

"It ain't gonna be too cozy, but it's better than nothin'," Tim added.

"Can I get you outta there?" Al leaned over John.

"Sure." John lifted himself up slightly and unbuckled the belts holding him in. "Help me to that tree over there and I'll sit against it for a while."

Al gently lifted John to his feet; John winced under the pain as he hobbled to the tree and collapsed under it.

"How do you feel?" Al asked.

"Like there's bleeding inside me," John paused. "I hope there's no infection in my gut where the bullet went through, I hope it was a clean shot."

"Billy found the slug," Tim interrupted. "He found it in a tree behind where you was standing when they shot at us."

Walking to where John was propped up, Billy stuck his hand into his pants pocket and rummaged around.

"Yeah, I saw a hole in a rotten tree trunk behind you, so I dug at it with my pocket knife." Billy pulled a flattened lead ball from his pocket. "You was shot with this ball, it had to be muskets they was shootin'."

John lifted up his hand and took the flattened lead projectile from Billy and examined it, turning it with his finger and thumb.

"It looks like red stains on it," John paused while still looking at the ball. "It's got to be my blood."

"Yeah, it is," Billy concurred. "You can keep it, to remember all this with."

"I think I'll remember it all anyway," John chuckled.

Billy tapped Tim on the shoulder and said, "Let's get the tent up, least ways as best we can."

Tim and Billy walked to the sling and began to untie it from the long wooden poles while Al sat beside John and leaned against the tree next to him.

"We'll get outta here by tomorrow, I know it." Al didn't know what else to say.

"I hope so," John said looking at the ever darkening sky.

"We sure were makin' a whole hell of a lot of noise out there today." Al stared towards the river.

"That we were." John nodded, acknowledging the obvious. "Anybody with half a brain, and half his hearing could find us today."

"We did shoot a few of them," Al's sounded serious. "Maybe they gave it a few more thoughts, I mean comin' after us."

"If they were army men, then they don't care, they'll be after us anyway," John said.

"I have to admit, this whole thing's got me wonderin' if this ain't sometime in the eighteen hundreds, or somethin' else like you said," Al sighed.

"I only said what I think, not what everybody else should think," John replied.

"I never did understand you when you got like this."

"Like what?"

"Talkin' like you're some sort of a educated fool or somethin'."

"I am an educated fool," John paused, "And so are we all."

Al laughed, "I guess you're right, this time."

Billy walked to John and Al and proclaimed, "We're finished with the tent, it ain't much, but it'll keep the snow off us tonight."

"You think it'll snow?" Al asked.

"Think?" Billy laughed. "I know."

"God, I hope it doesn't get too cold tonight," John moaned. "I'm cold enough as it is, in between burning up."

"We got to keep him as warm as we can tonight," Tim said. "He's been bounced around so much today, we don't know what's happened inside where the bullet went through."

"Don't lift my spirits too much." John grinned nervously.

"Y'all know what I mean," Tim stammered.

176

"Yeah, we do." Al put his hand on John's shoulder. "We also need to keep our guns dry."

"How much ammo do y'all have? That may be important real soon," Billy asked.

"Might be." Tim looked in his coat pocket. "I got two boxes total."

"That's forty, right?" Billy asked.

"Yeah," Tim answered.

"I got only thirty two left in all," Billy said. "I shot up a bunch back at camp."

"Well, now that you ask, all I have is sixteen loaded cartridges left." Al answered. "But I've brought my little hand loader, 'n the stuff for it."

"What caliber?" Billy asked quickly.

"30-06, that's the same as John shoots, but none of the rest of you," Al answered.

"How much powder, 'n how many bullets 'n primers?" Billy asked.

"Enough for 'bout twenty five or so reloads," Al paused. "I saved my brass from this morning, 'n I'll reload 'em tonight."

"How much ammo you got?" Billy looked at John.

"I brought one bandolier of full clips, plus two in the modified clip I use to keep the game warden happy," John answered.

"So, how many is that?" Billy asked.

"There's six full clips of eight in the bandolier, plus two, so that's fifty rounds in all," John replied.

"I always did wonder why you brought that ol' Garand on these hunts," Billy scoffed.

"It works fine, besides it's the newest rifle I've got," John sounded defensive.

"But it's so old," Billy snorted.

John propped himself up straight to see Billy, "But right now it's the only military rifle, and the only semi-automatic we've got."

177

"He's right," Tim agreed. "If we're in a fire fight, his rifle'll be better than any of ours, and he shoots what Al can reload."

Al chimed in, "I used one of those when I was in ROTC in high school and I can say that's one hell of a rifle for a fire fight, if we have one."

"Yeah," Billy acquiesced. "I guess it could come in handy. How many rounds you got in your forty four, Al?"

"Twelve," Al sounded apologetic and shrugged. "I wasn't expectin' to be in this mess."

"None of us were," John said. "How much cooked meat do we have?"

"I stuffed your pack with what we had left." Tim opened the top of John's pack and pulled out several pieces of cooked deer meat. "Do you think we should try a fire tonight?"

"No way," Billy insisted.

"I agree," Al added. "If anyone's still near here, they'll see it 'n we won't stand a chance if they mean to harm us."

"Hell," Billy sounded incredulous. "They mean to kill us."

"Well." Tim handed the meat out to the others. "Let's eat cold meat 'n get to sleep."

"How about a can of beans too?" Billy asked. "I could use some variety, you know."

"Sure," Al chuckled. "So long as you promise not to fart too much in the tent."

"It ain't as air tight as it used to be," Billy chortled. "So don't complain so much tonight."

"Someone oughtta stand guard while the rest of us sleep," Al suggested.

"Let's take turns," Tim said. "I'll go first, after dark."

"That's okay with me." Billy took another bite of his cold meal.

All four of the men ate in silence; they stared out at the darkening forest around them, and the softly flowing river beside them.

"The leafless branches below the sight horizon look like a brownish gray fog." John lay back against the tree. "It's getting dark, and the branches look like a fog rising off the forest bed."

"I don't know 'bout that, but look at this." Billy pointed to several small flakes of snow falling quietly to the ground.

"Just what we need." Tim slowly rose to his feet. "I'm goin' to the river 'n draw some water before it gets too slippery."

"Be careful," Al advised.

Al walked the short distance to the road and began pacing, looking as intensely as he could through the darkness.

"You were right, Billy, it is snowing." John had slipped down to a prone position, laying on his back.

"Yeah," Billy replied. "Are you all right, I mean really all right?"

"No, I hurt like hell, and I think I need to get to a hospital soon or I'll bleed to death," John said flatly.

"Why don't you take some aspirin?" Billy asked. "I got some in my pack.

"Aspirin thins the blood." John answered. "I'd bleed to death sooner."

"Oh."

"Al has some Tylenol Threes, but I'm trying to space them out since he only had six of them."

"If you're right, there ain't no hospital; I mean, if we're in the eighteen hundreds there ain't gonna be no hospital," Billy said.

"I know what you mean."

"Yeah," Billy paused, looking at the river for several minutes in silence. "Why do you collect all those old junky guns?"

"I collect military antiques," John answered. "All of them are working examples of what man used to kill his fellow creatures for the past two centuries. More effort is spent on that quest than any other; it shows, in a macabre sense, the best of man's ingenuity. Like any piece of machinery, you can see forever the genius of the man who invented it. It's as if his

179

thoughts live in his creation. I've always felt that mechanical inventions are an execution of thought as written and spoken languages are, that's why I collect mechanical watches too."

"Yeah, what's with that?"

"That's what Janice asks too," John sounded thoughtful for a second, then grinned again. "She says I like to collect time and death and I suppose the two are connected in some cosmic way."

"Whatever; what I asked was why do you spend so much time 'n money collectin' old guns?"

John moved to his side, audibly showing the pain he felt.

"I don't know, why do you abuse the only woman who'd love you no matter what?"

"That's none of your damn business," Billy said loudly. "Everybody always says I knock her around too much, hell, I don't give her nothin' she don't ask for."

"Nobody asks to be beaten up, nobody asks to be humiliated." John took a deep breath. "Nobody asks to be shot."

"And I sure as hell didn't ask for this lecture." Billy sat back down next to John.

"And I'm not doing it as a request, but I'm going to do it none the less."

"Yeah," Billy spoke softly, taking in a deep breath and letting it out forcefully, making a small cloud of steam rise in front of his face. "I can't help it, she can get me madder than anyone else, she gets under my skin deeper than I can stand."

"The passion's there, don't lose it by telling yourself it's something else." John put his hand on Billy's arm and patted it.

"What do you mean?"

"I haven't told the others yet, but Janice and I finalized our divorce last month."

"No, I didn't even know you two was havin' no troubles, you two always seemed to get along so well." Billy sat up straight and leaned away from John. "What happened?"

180

"The feeling left, it left both of us, it was like I didn't recognize myself anymore and Janice didn't know me either. It hit me like a meteor; I didn't belong anywhere anymore, not here, not with her and I existed without connections to hold me down," John said.

John stared at the river, then returned his gaze to Billy.

"Listen to what I said," John continued. "You and Darlene have the passion still, the desire for each other and the zeal for life so don't mistake it for anger and jealousy and risk losing it; see it for what it is and hold on to it for dear life because that's exactly what it is."

Billy stared at John for a moment, then he took a deep breath, "You and Janice?" He softly expelled his breath. "Who has your daughter? Janice?"

"She'll share both our homes. Janice moved in with some of her people, near where her ancestors once lived."

"Where's that?"

"Not far from me."

"God, It's cold here," Billy shivered.

"And, getting colder."

Tim came sliding back up the bank with a pot full of water, splashing over the sides. The closer he came to John and Billy, the more they could make out his condition; mud covered his whole right side, and river water dripped from almost all his clothes.

"You fell in?" Billy couldn't contain his delight in someone else's discomfort.

"Funny," Tim scowled.

"You'd better get out of those wet clothes, or Al and Billy will be carrying both of us tomorrow." John propped himself back up.

Al, hearing the noise, came walking back into the camp area.

"What happened?" Al stared at Tim. "Get out of those clothes right now."

"I've got one extra set of long johns," Billy said.

181

"I think between all of us, we can get him dry, except for his boots and without a fire, there ain't no way to dry them boots," Al said.

"So, what am I supposed to do?" Tim shrugged his shoulders.

"I've got one can of Sterno I was savin'," Al reluctantly said. "I guess this qualifies as an emergency. I'm going to get my reloading stuff, 'n I'll get the Sterno too."

"But," Billy sounded serious. "Keep the flame hidden from the road, in case someone walks by tonight."

"Yeah, I'll do it," Tim replied.

"And don't catch your boots on fire, neither."

Darkness completely covered the river side camp. The wind was not with them that night, but the snow was; it fell, silently, in larger and larger flakes, covering everything with a fresh white coat of crystals. Tim sat huddled over a small blue flame, passing a wet boot through the heat. Inside the lean-to tent, John lay on his left side, Billy sat by the front opening and Al sat inside, next to John.

"At least the snow'll cover our tracks." Al looked to the front of the tent.

"Yeah," Billy grunted.

"I hope Tim can get his boots dry," John mumbled, not wanting to say anything else.

The three men fell silent for the next five minutes while the large snow flakes made soft thumps on the top of the make shift tent.

"Somethin's been eatin' at me," Al spoke in a loud whisper.

"What?" John asked.

"What that man who shot at us today yelled."

"What?" Billy chimed in.

"He said, and boy can I remember it, 'die you bastard'."

"Yeah, I remember that too," Billy sounded puzzled. "Why did he say that, why did he shoot at us, and give you one hell of a lick? We ain't nothin' to him. I could understand a bunch of yahoos tryin' to rob us, but I don't think they was. Maybe they thought we was Yankees and he's still fightin' the war after all these years."

"If those guys were from the eighteen hundreds, then why'd they want to kill us? We're from the South, all of us, even John, least ways his folks were then," Al paused. "We're white, 'n we're Southerners, so why'd they want to shoot at us?"

"Perhaps they saw us as something else, not as we are now," John guessed.

"What does that mean?" Billy turned to him and asked.

"If we're stuck in the past, what do we look like to someone from this time?" John lay back down. "Who knows what they saw when they shot at us. Hell, I wonder what I'll see the next time I look into the mirror, that is if I ever get the chance again."

"So what," Al said. "We're folks, like them, I don't care what you say, they're just like us 'n they shouldn't have shot at us."

John looked into Al's eyes, "That might be true but we could be dreaming all this too, although my part of the dream sure hurts like hell."

"It could be we is still back at the van wreck 'n we's all dreamin' the same thing," Billy added.

"Funny you should mention that," John said. "Tim mentioned that same thing the other night."

"It makes sense," Billy replied.

"I don't know what's goin' on." Al looked to the ground. "Not anymore, I don't know what's goin' on no more."

"All I know is what I see," Billy said.

"That's what I'm sayin'," Al sounded bewildered.

"The trouble with that is that I don't know what I'm seein'," Billy replied. "Most of it feels real, but none of it makes sense."

"Everything makes sense as long as you find the right frame of reference," John added.

183

"Ain't no frame of reference I like that makes someone shoot John." Al looked back at Billy.

"You suppose they shot only John for some reason?" Billy asked.

"He happened to be the first one they shot, that's all," Al said. "They was shootin' at all of us, if we're in the eighteen hundreds then either the war's bein' fought or has just been fought, 'n they'll shoot at anyone they don't know."

"But," Billy said. "We ain't got no uniforms on so how the hell could they know who we are?"

Al responded, "Neither did they, exactly, remember, they was all wearin' old timey clothes, and only some of them had rebel hats on; no one could think what we had on were uniforms."

"What about the orange vests?" John asked, staring straight up.

"Yeah." Al scratched his chin. "I guess so."

"What if this' the present, and those yahoos shootin' at us are a motorcycle gang, wantin' to rob us like I said?" Billy asked.

"With muskets and not MAC 10s?" John asked.

"Could be, but I guess not." Billy shook his head.

"Maybe they saw us as our ancestors were, and not as we are now." Al brightened up as he thought of that idea.

"That's a good thought," John agreed with him. "Go on with it."

"I thought that if any of our ancestors was Yankees, or somethin' they didn't like," Al paused, looking at Billy. "Well, maybe they saw us as that, 'n shot at us."

"What the hell are we?" Billy demanded. "I'm a damn good 'ol Southern boy, 'n all my kin was before me."

"It's a thought." Al looked at the ground.

"I like the idea." John turned his head towards Al. "They see something in my background that makes me an enemy, or somebody else has an ancestor who wasn't one of the good old boys back then?"

184

"Like I said." Billy glared at John. "I ain't got nothin' but relations to be damn proud of."

"Well." Al hesitated. "My mom's folks came down here from Indiana, they might've thought I was a Yankee."

"That's it," Billy said in a delighted tone.

"My mother's folks came from Massachusetts," John said. "But my father's side of the family originated from here, my grandfather came from this state."

"Maybe someone's blood ain't so pure, if you know what I mean." Billy cast a glance at John, then at Al.

"No," John sighed. "Tell us what you mean."

"You know." Billy half smiled. "The white cell count ain't too high."

"You know, Billy." John rose back up on his two elbows. "You really are a horse's ass."

"Okay," Billy indignantly replied. "I'm an ass, but what're you?"

"I'm a human being, but I'm beginning to wonder what you are," John answered him.

"I think this' gone far enough," Al spoke up. "A man's what he is, not what his past kin was."

"He is what his kin was, in this damned place anyway," Billy insisted.

"The way I see it, it doesn't matter," John said slowly. "We belong here, on this land, no more or no less than the men who shot me."

"What you getting at?" Al asked.

"Other creatures belong with the land; humans can become aware of it that way, the land as part of our body, part of our being. But it takes hundreds of generations to do that. None of us here have grown that way with this land, only the Indians had that relationship with this place. Those of us left here are alone, apart from this spot, all of us."

"You're gettin' weird again." Billy shook his head.

185

"There's a feeling about all this." John ignored Billy's comment. "Whether we're dreaming or dead, this place is communicating with us."

"Great," Billy snorted "Now he's got talking dirt."

Again ignoring Billy's protestations, John still spoke evenly, "This place is a part and player in all this; those people out there are like us, they're lost with no sign of home."

"They don't look lost to me, they know enough about this place to find us and shoot us," Al said.

John slid back down onto the ground, "Maybe it's me they're after."

"I think this has gone too far, we're gettin' silly now." Al sounded frustrated.

"Look," Billy insisted. "We've been shot at, 'n we're runnin' for our lives, all I want is to know why."

"And?" John asked.

"And," Billy continued. "If I get killed I want to know who I'm dyin' for."

"If I die, I'll know I died helping my friends to survive," Al quickly replied.

"Yeah, yeah," Billy sounded exasperated. "But I don't know who I'm fighting for anymore, I mean, who are any of you?"

"We all know what you're driving at, Billy." John looked at Billy as he stared out the flap of the tent. "But, almost everybody who's lived in the south for more than five generations has some black relatives, somewhere."

Billy snapped his head around and stared at John. "I ain't. Is that why Janice left you?"

All three men fell silent, their eyes quietly exchanging questions. Billy turned from the others and sat, staring through the flap in the tent. Al arched his eyebrows in an expression of surprise towards John.

"You and Janice?" Al asked.

"We couldn't find any common ground between us, or I guess we lost all our common ground. I still love her so much

186

that I'd trade one hundred of these wounds to have her back." John sniffed and tried to swallow the growing lump in his throat. "But, something stopped happening, but I don't know what."

"To me, you two were happy together," Al sympathized. "It'll be better when you get back."

"I don't think so." John wiped his cheek. "I'd give anything for another chance, but I don't think so."

Billy moved to one side and let Tim into the tent; Tim sat next to John and put his hand on his shoulder.

"I heard," Tim said. "I'm sorry."

"It's all right." John cleared his throat. "We need to think about what to do right here, and right now."

"You're right," Tim replied. "Right now, I'll put my semi-dry boots on and stand watch while the rest of you try to get some sleep."

"That sounds like a damn good idea," Al said.

"I'll wake Billy up when it's his turn." Tim climbed out of the tent and tied the flap shut.

Chapter 17

'Tis all a Chequer-board of Nights and Days
Where Destiny with Men for Pieces plays:
Hither and thither moves, and mates and slays,
And one by one back in the Closet lays.
Omar Khayyám The Rubáiyát of Omar Khayyám

That night it snowed for only a few hours, then a strong, fast cold front moved through, clearing the skies. The wind picked up mightily from the northwest, making the sides of the makeshift tent to flap in the streaming cold, until the tent resembled a tattered sail on a floundering tall mast frigate in a North Sea gale. The mass of cold air that covered the forest acted as a clear lens, to magnify the stars and quarter moon. Their faint light made everything glow from its own inner fire.

Tim gently stuffed his hand over Al's mouth and shook him to consciousness.

"What." Al's voice was muffled by Tim's hand.

"Quiet," Tim whispered to Al, lifting a finger to his lips to silence Billy who had opened his eyes.

"What the hell's goin' on?" Billy said in a loud whisper.

"I said shut up," Tim whispered quietly back, this time holding up his palm to Billy's face. "There's a whole column of men out there, marchin' down the road."

"What?" Al whispered.

"Get your guns, 'n meet me out there, but be quiet," Tim whispered. "Someone wake up John to make sure he don't make no noise for a while."

"I'll do it," Al replied.

"Fine." Billy pulled on his boots and coat, then crawled out of the tent with his rifle.

188

"John." Al shook his friend.

"I heard." John turned to Al and opened his eyes. "Take my rifle, it'll be better than yours in case you all have to fight."

Al looked at John for a moment, then silently took his Garand and bandoleer of clips.

"How's the pain?" Al whispered.

"Better." John looked up at Al as he headed out the tent. "I might make it after all."

Al duck-walked slowly, taking care not to crunch leaves or twigs, until he reached the other two men who were stretched out on their stomachs looking at the road. He dropped silently beside them and peered through the bushes to the road.

A line of hundreds of men, all dressed in ragged clothes, half in gray uniforms, half in mostly farm clothes, dragged along the snowy path, all heading up river. The column moved silently. Each man carried a long musket; some had their rifles strapped on their backs, others shouldered theirs, some gripped their muskets in one hand.

The gray men looked translucent in the starlight, almost as if they had died, and not realizing it, marched towards another battle which would never come in a war that would never end.

The column passed in front of the three men staring from the bushes, until the last gray soul disappeared around the bend in the road and into the dark forest. The crunching of boots in the snow grew fainter, finally becoming lost in the rush of the wind.

"What did you make of that?" Tim asked, still staring ahead.

"If I didn't know better, it looked like a bunch of tired defeated rebel soldiers comin' back from a war which ended a lot longer ago than I care to remember." Al turned to look at Billy. "Maybe they was lost."

"Shit." Billy slowly shook his head. "That weird ass hole back there's right, we's a hundred and fifty some years in the past for sure, but how the hell do we get outta here?"

189

"We go to where we know," Al answered. "We go to where the road crosses the river, then we head to the city, we'll know where we are then."

"I'm scared," Tim said. "What if that town's in the eighteen hundreds, what do we do then?"

"I've been thinkin' 'bout that the last day or two," Billy interrupted. "If we're back that far in the past, we could use what we know 'bout history to make a fortune. Think 'bout it, we all know how a car works, 'n how an airplane works, we could all make a fortune." He continued unraveling his scheme, but the others shook their heads.

"We don't belong here," Tim insisted. "We've gotta be breakin' some law of nature if we are back in time, if what we saw the last twelve hours is really what we think it is."

"Listen you two." Al sat up and brushed the snow off his coat and pants. "We still could be lettin' our imaginations run wild. Let's go on what we know for sure. John needs a doctor real soon, 'n we've got to get him outta here at first light."

"Should we try to catch up with those soldiers, 'n ask them for help?" Tim asked. "At least they might have some medicine."

"We've got as much as they do; they didn't have no medicine back then that would do him no more good than what we have."

Billy looked down both directions of the road. "Besides, they're the ones who want us dead, remember?"

"Get back down," Al insisted. "They might still have scouts on the road."

Billy sat back down on the snow and sulked. "Don't get so huffy."

"I'm worried 'bout John," Tim said. "Ain't there nothin' we can do for him?"

"If somethin's tore up inside him, only a doctor in a hospital can sew it back up right. Other than that, all we can do is keep him warm, fed, 'n give him enough water to drink," Billy said.

190

"Billy's right, that's all we can do for him; keep him as comfortable as we can and get him outta here," Al added. "Let's get back in there."

"I'll keep watch now," Billy said. "What time is it?"

"It's three in the morning." Tim handed Billy his poncho. "Here, take this, it'll cut the wind for you."

"Thanks."

Billy took the plastic rain poncho and wrapped himself in it as he nestled behind the bush next to the road. When Tim and Al crept back, they found John was sitting up and drinking water from a pot near the rear of the tent.

"This water had a skim of ice over it." John turned to face the two men crawling into the tent. "How's the weather out there, as cold as it is in here?"

"Colder," Al answered.

"Yeah," Tim added. "The sky cleared off 'bout an hour ago, 'n the wind picked up somethin' bad."

"I hear and feel it in here too." John shivered. "Is Billy taking the watch now?"

"Yeah," Tim answered.

"Do you suppose I could use his sleeping bag while he's out there?" John asked.

"Sure, are you real cold?" Al asked.

"Damn cold," John answered. "What went on out there?"

"We saw a couple hundred or so men march down the road," Tim answered. "They looked real tired, 'n cold, like us."

"Were they dressed like the one who shot me?" John asked.

"Yeah, they was," Al answered. "They looked like they'd been through hell."

John looked at Al, then at Tim. "You said the obvious, Al."

"Don't think that hasn't crossed my mind too." Tim stared into John's eyes.

191

"Well." John lay back down. "Dead men don't get up in the morning, so let's get to sleep and see if we do."

Al lay down inside his sleeping bag. Tim silently slipped into his bag, lay on his back and rested his head on the palms of his hands.

"You're right, Al," Tim whispered.

"'Bout what?" Al asked.

"'Bout gettin' back to where we know."

"Good night, Tim." Al quietly turned on his side and fell asleep in a few brief seconds.

"Are you still awake, Tim?" John whispered.

"Yeah."

"If something happens to me." John paused while he took several long breaths. "Could you tell Janice what happened, I want you to tell her."

"I'm sorry that you and Janice got a divorce, that's somethin' I never thought could happen." Tim sat up and leaned towards John's head. "Why did you go through with it? Neither of you'll never find nobody that'll be as good."

"I know that, it was my fault."

"Did you get another woman?" Tim asked reproachfully.

"No, were it only that simple, I could have done something about that and we could have stayed together."

"Has she got someone else?"

"No," John paused. "She hasn't."

"You ain't queer or nothin', are you?" Tim asked.

John smiled and silently shook his head.

"Well, then it ain't lost, you two could find each other again, give it some time."

John looked startled. "Find each other again, give it some time," he repeated the words as if he were tasting them. "I never thought of that. It's been staring me in the face; find each other again, find each other again in some other time, damnit, I know what this is all about now, it all makes sense, everything in life makes sense if you only look at it in the right context."

192

"What did I say?" Tim asked. "None of this makes sense to me."

"I'll find her again." John paused for a moment. "My father spoke to us; the hospital listed his time of death at the same hour and minute he came to our house, so far away from the hospital."

"I remember you told me about it before," Tim sounded confused. "What about it?"

"He told me about his father." The corner of John's mouth began to form a smile. "His father grew up on this land, but the time wasn't right for him. He thought he wasn't part of the land even though he was. He was lost, and all of us, the whole family's been lost since then. What didn't happen then, could happen again, I can make a difference, I know I can."

"I don't know what you're talking about, John."

"What we were talking about the other night," John sounded more awake. "What if we're dreaming this, then whose dream is it?"

"Yeah," Tim sounded groggy.

"It has to be my dream." John relaxed back into his sleeping bags. "Why else would I be the one shot."

"Whatever, John." Tim tried to sound consoling, but his voice came out frustrated. "I don't know what you're talkin' about, but it ain't no never mind, you need some rest."

"All I said was that you've given me the answer, everything is going to be all right." John relaxed his muscles as best as he could. "It all can be undone, and done again."

"That's the spirit." Tim gingerly patted his arm. "Now get some sleep, I want you to tell Janice what happened yourself."

"I shall." John fell into a painful sleep.

Chapter 18

The miserable have no other medicine
But only hope.
William Shakespeare Measure for Measure, act 3, sc. 1

The night wind heaped an abundance of snow against the northern face of the tent and blocked the early morning light on that side. The partially open ends, and the loose side let most of the heat generated by the people inside the tent escape unfelt by the bare portions of their bodies.

Al awoke first, cold and hungry; still tightly wrapped in his sleeping bag, he moved on his elbows to John's side and looked at his wounded friend. He watched John draw a deep, steady breath, then breathe out. Al pulled a hand from his sleeping bag and put it on John's arm.

"Are you awake?"

John moved slightly and started to roll on his left side. He stopped after a short movement, winced, and let out a muffled grunt. When he opened his eyes, Al's face hovered a few inches from his.

"I am now."

"How do you feel?"

Tim opened his eyes, turned his head towards John and remained still.

"I hurt, but I think something's going right inside me."

"How do you mean?" Tim asked.

"I haven't been able to take a leak since I got shot, even though I've been drinking a hell of a lot of water." John gulped and cleared his throat. "I was afraid one or both of my kidneys had shut down."

"But?" Al asked. "Now?"

194

"Now I have to piss like crazy." John struggled to sit up. "Can one of you help me outside to pee?"

Al laughed, and Tim answered John with a nod.

"Get your jacket on first, then I'll take you to your appointed rounds," Tim happily responded.

Al helped John get his boots and jacket on, then he and Tim eased John to the outside and propped him against a tree. Tim wandered off to locate Billy while Al waited for John to finish.

"Can you manage alone?" Al asked.

"I think so."

John took his right glove off, arranged himself, then began to urinate. "Shit," he whispered quietly to himself. A bright red liquid spattered on the snow in front of him. He finished, zipped himself up and put his glove back on, then he slowly pivoted on the tree and came face to face with Al, who was staring at the pool of blood on the ground.

"John." Al's expression was half way between shock and tears. "We got to get you to some kind of hospital, today."

"I know," John softly spoke. "I know."

"Come over here," Tim called.

Al helped John to where Tim stood; the three men looked at Billy who had fallen asleep bundled under his coat and Tim's poncho, only his head and one of his boots clearly showed.

"Why don't I make a loud noise 'n see what he does?" Tim chuckled.

"He might shoot you, that's what he might do." Al looked seriously at Tim.

"I guess," Tim sighed. "Hey, Billy." Tim shouted.

The sleeping form shook slightly, then harder.

"I musta fell asleep," Billy moaned, then he yawned. "How's John?"

"Not so good," Al replied. "If we don't get him to a hospital today, he might not get outta here in one piece."

"I might not make it out of here at all," John added.

195

"What 'bout them soldiers?" Billy walked to the tent and pulled out the back pack with the meat in it. "What we gonna do if they's up ahead?"

"We'll do whatever it takes to get John to a hospital," Al insisted.

"I guess you're right." Billy bit into a piece of the remaining deer meat. "Hell, this stuff's frozen."

"So are we all," John said. "Let's get going as soon as we can."

"Yeah," Tim chimed in.

Tim pulled out a piece of meat and handed it to Al, he then pulled out another piece of meat and held it in his hands.

"Let's eat and hit the road. That crossing can't be much further on up the road from here, 'n we've got to see something familiar up there," Billy said.

"You want somethin' to eat?" Al looked at John, who sat back down on a fallen tree.

"No, I'll take some water when we get to a place that's not too steep to draw it from the river."

"Okay, I'll get the tent down, 'n you and Billy make up the sling for John," Tim said.

"Wait 'till I finish my deer-cicle," Billy said in an annoyed tone.

"I figure it can't be much more than another two miles 'til the bridge," Al said. "And that crossin's been there since the early eighteen hundreds."

"So?" Billy asked. "What then? The nearest town in that direction is a good twenty miles at least."

"We'll cross that bridge when we come to it," John laughed.

"Funny," Billy chuckled back at John. "We'll get you outta here no matter what," he paused. "It's that I hate surprises."

"Me too," Tim said.

196

Al, Tim and Billy silently broke camp; they reconstructed the sling, and placed John in it. This time they bundled John in one of the sleeping bags, then strapped him into the sling.

"The snow's not too deep," Tim observed.

"Most of it blew off the road last night," Billy added.

"I wish the wind would die down today." John shivered. "It might not feel so cold then."

"The cold's in your head," Tim remarked to John. "Try pulling me for a while 'n then it won't feel so cold."

The column of four men walked for another two miles in silence; they stopped only to draw water from the river at the outside edge of a gentle bend which presented them with a narrow sandy area on which to stand.

As the sun rose further in the sky, the temperature stopped falling, but the wind blew harder. Animal sounds faded in the wind, only an occasional crow call echoed by the river. Most of the ground animals remained sheltered from the weather.

Billy, Al and Tim kept a careful watch on the road ahead of them, behind them, as well as the forest beside them. They stopped at half mile intervals to listen for following footsteps in the woods; the sounds of the wind and the forest were their only company.

"Damn bridge should be here somewhere," Al sighed.

"What's that?" Tim pointed to a dark brown structure ahead on the bank of the river.

The men stopped, then Tim lay John in his sling on the ground. Billy walked to the head of the group and took his loaded rifle off his shoulder and held it in front of him.

"Here, Al." John lifted his rifle from beside him. "Take this and give me yours."

"Sure."

Al stepped back and exchanged rifles; he loaded a cartridge into the chamber and moved next to Billy.

"You go through the woods, Tim 'n me'll head straight to it, next to the river 'n off the road," Al said.

"Sounds good to me." Billy moved quickly to the forest, then crouched down and slowly walked towards the unknown area ahead of them.

Tim and Al pulled John off to the forest side of the road and placed him behind a tree.

"It looks familiar to me now," John said softly.

"What does? Al asked.

"These woods, I think we're almost there," John said.

"Where?" Tim cocked his head.

"Home."

"You wait here."

Al laid his hand on John's shoulder, wondering about the state of his friend's mind. Tim and Al walked across the road, then up an almost unused animal trail along the bank of the river.

"Look at that." Tim pointed to a man's body laying next to a raft made of logs, pulled onto the bank of the river.

Al stared at the man laying on the ground for a moment before he spoke, "Do ya think he's dead?"

"Yeah," Tim slowly said. "But be careful, somebody's shot him, 'n they might still be somewhere 'round here."

"Look," Al said in a loud whisper. "There's Billy, walkin' right up to the body."

"Let's wait here for a second," Tim said. "Let's see if anyone else comes up there."

Billy squatted next to the man on the ground, took his glove off and placed his hand on the man's neck. He slowly took his hand away from the man's neck, and stood up, looking all around the site, then he motioned to Tim and Al to join him.

"You go on," Al said to Tim. "I'll go back 'n get John."

Tim walked to Billy, looking in all directions as he moved slowly to the body, sprawled face down in the snow.

"How long's he been dead?" Tim asked.

"Since last night at least," Billy replied. "His body's froze stiff."

"What is this place?"

"Looks to me like this' our bridge." Billy looked across the river. "Look there." Billy pointed to the opposite bank. "See, that's where the road continues on to the city."

"Yeah." Tim strained to read a small sign on the other side of the river, beside the road. "There's a sign pointing to the city with the mileage next to it."

"Look there." Billy pointed to a rope, tied to a tree and disappearing into the swiftly flowing river. "This was a ferry to get you across; he got you on the raft 'n then he pulled the raft over on the rope that used to be attached to that pulley across the river."

"Yeah." Al pulled John to the site. "I see what you mean; do ya think the soldiers killed him last night?"

"It don't matter," Billy answered. "What does matter, is that we can't get back to the city by way of that road," he paused, looking at the water in the river. "I ain't gonna swim across, are you? And, there's no main road goin' up stream on this side of the river. I guess we could walk up stream on this side of the river, but it wanders all over the damn place,."

"Well, what bright idea do you have then?" Al asked.

"Hey," Tim called from a few paces away. "Look at this."

Tim pointed to another small hand lettered wooden sign, nailed to a tree beside a narrow path leading into the forest.

"What's the Rose Community?" Billy asked, looking at the sign.

"It was a small farming community that began before 1850." John propped himself up on his elbows to see down the small dirt path. "Don't you guys remember the historical marker? It's real close to where we hunt, it's on that dirt road we never go down."

"I don't know what the hell you're talkin' about," Billy insisted.

"It's at the end of the road which parallels the ridge we hunt on sometimes, it twists around and ends up back on the river further down from there," John said patiently.

199

"Yeah." Al's face brightened. "I remember goin' there once; there ain't nothin left but a few foundations. The Forest Service's chained off the ruins but I never stopped to read the sign there that tells you 'bout it."

"I read it, it tells 'bout the people who started it. They was named Rose, that's where it got its name from. Maybe it's still got people in it now, or what ever time we're in," Tim said. "Let's go there for help."

"They ran a mill," John added. "Like that boy told you two nights ago."

"Yeah," Billy sounded as if he remembered something important. "That was his last name, Mark Rose."

"Does that sound like a clue as to which way to go?" John asked.

"Right now I don't give a damn where we go, so long as we go somewhere," Billy said with a sour expression.

"What do the rest of you think?" Al asked, looking at each of the other men.

"We can't get across the river, and it's for sure we ain't in the same time we started this trip," Tim sounded reconciled. "So, why not go down this road?"

"Billy?" Al asked.

"Fine with me, what 'bout you?" Billy looked back at Al.

Al looked down at John, "What do you think? You're the one with the most at stake in this."

John fell back from his elbows on to the ground.

"Amid the gold of the eternal rose, whose gradual leaves, unfolding, fragrantly extol that sun which spring for aye bestows," John said to no one in particular.

Al looked up to Tim, who returned his stare and Billy looked down at John.

"What the hell're you talkin' 'bout?" Billy demanded.

"I said, let's go to the Rose Community, it's home to me again." John replied. "The sign says it's only a mile from here, so let's get moving."

200

"You aren't making much sense, John." Tim joined the conversation.

"Time isn't a straight line, it's more of a mosaic of bits and pieces in random order, made real by perception," John said. "I don't know whether this is the way to heaven or hell, I do know it's a way home."

Billy shook his head in confusion, then said, "You never do make sense half the time and I'm beginin' to think you lost most of your brains when that bullet went through you."

"Lift him up and let's get walking," Al said harshly at Billy, then looked at John. "Here." He pulled John's rifle from his shoulder. "Let's swap, mine's lighter."

"Sure."

Billy lifted John and fell in behind Al, who had already begun to walk the small dirt road ahead; Tim followed John, and kept a close watch on him.

"You got your wish," Tim said to John.

"What's that?" John looked surprised.

"The wind's died down 'n it feels warmer," Tim said.

"You're right." John winced from pain as he moved to get more comfortable.

"Are you all right?" Tim asked.

"No," John paused for a long moment. "I think I'm dying."

"Don't even think that," Tim insisted. "You ain't gonna die on us, not here, 'n not yet."

"I feel I have unfinished business here." John fell silent and closed his eyes. "I now know what my father told me, it makes sense now."

"What are you talkin' about?" Tim cocked his head slightly as he remembered the previous conversation. "Oh, yeah, what did he tell you?"

"It was his father, my grandfather, who lived right here. My dad said he never faced his life's battle and fought it."

Tim looked at John for a moment, without recognition, then lay his hand on John's shoulder.

201

"You try to get some rest, we'll get you some help from somewhere real soon," Tim said.

Tim watched John as he tried to sleep, bouncing in the sling as Billy pulled it along the rutted dirt road. After a mile of bouncing in the sling, John finally managed to fall asleep.

"What if the men we saw last night are up there?" Billy asked.

"I don't give a shit anymore," Al answered, looking straight ahead. "We have to get John some help soon; I'd deal with the devil himself right now if I had to."

"We may already have," Tim muttered to himself.

Five minutes passed as they steadily walked in silence.

"We had to have hunted in these woods, but I don't recognize a damned thing," Billy broke the stillness.

"John's asleep," Tim quietly replied.

"Oh," Billy spoke in a quieter voice. "I still don't recognize a thing, we should be real close to where we have hunted a bunch of times, if this is where John said it was."

"It is," Al interrupted. "And I don't recognize anything either, but we may be somewhere else in time, like John said."

"That's a first for you, Al." Tim stopped walking and stared at him.

"Hell, I'd believe the sky's green right now if it would help us get outta here quicker with John," Al replied.

"Me too," Tim said softly.

Chapter 19

The Upper Valley of the Connecticut River encompasses three states, Northern Massachusetts, Western New Hampshire and Eastern Vermont. Early in the history of European settlement, families moved north from the Connecticut and Massachusetts colonies on the Connecticut River to build new lives on useable farming land. Later, manufacturing bloomed along the waterway.

The Barrington family traced their American lineage back to a blacksmith who arrived in New Hartford, Connecticut from Shropshire, England in 1697. By the late eighteenth century, the Barrington family were nearly all involved in some sort of manufacturing endeavor. Ralph's ancestors manufactured clocks, and clock parts in three small factories in Massachusetts. Around 1820, the family decided to open a fourth factory in Bennington, Vermont to manufacture clock and watch springs to feed their own plants as well as sell to other clock and watch makers. Ralph Barrington's father served as the owner and president of the Barrington Spring Company as soon as the facility was completed in 1822.

The Barrington family accepted Paul, even though he was a bastard child; no one ever shunned him, nor did any family member hold a grudge. Ralph Barrington traveled the country buying land for only four years after his son Paul joined him.

Previously, in 1866, after Ralph had mustered out of the Army, he had spent two years at the family factory with his own father, but he soon tired of that career and sought another. Through family connections, Ralph became a land purchasing agent for six wealthy speculators in Boston and New York City. But after years of travel, in 1885, he returned home with Paul. Ralph took over the family manufacturing plant in Bennington, which prospered. Ralph died prematurely of pneumonia in 1891.

Ralph married soon after he found Paul and three years before he settled down as the owner of the plant; he and his wife had four children. Although Ralph's children by his marriage inherited most of his wealth and the watch spring plant, Paul inherited the family summer home. The Barrington family felt this was the proper legacy for an illegitimate son; he was a good friend and confidant to them his entire life.

While traveling with his father, Paul had made his own land investments. He was careful with his money. He also invested in several western railroad companies; some of those investments proved foolish, but most paid off exceptionally well.

Paul married well, his wife was the eldest daughter of a banking family who owned six banks in Massachusetts and Vermont. They had one son, Scott, born a year after they married in 1896.

As Summer in the American South is relentless and debilitating, so is Winter in the Upper Connecticut Valley. But Summer is gentle in the north woods. If January is the bitterest month, July is the kindest and after the black flies disappear, most Summer afternoons are inviting. The Barrington house stayed busy with summer family visitors. Overlooking the Connecticut River, it had been the family summer home for three generations.

With three stories, eight bedrooms and three large summer porches, it was more than enough for the waves of Barringtons who invaded in June and left in September. In 1891, right before he died, Ralph willed it to Paul, who, along with his wife and child, settled into it as their permanent residence.

Over the next two decades, stresses of a wartime economy put Paul in a bad financial condition. In the summer of 1918, he suffered a series of small strokes. He was only fifty three years old; his wife felt the financial stress was causing the strokes.

Paul had never told his son, Scott, about his first sixteen years of life; he never felt the time was right. But one summer night he wondered if perhaps time was running out. He called his son into the bedroom, where he lay propped up against the bed's headboard.

"I'm going to die, although I feel it's not yet my time to die, I've not had near enough time on this earth to do everything I wanted but I guess that's all the time the Lord has given me. They've been good years, especially since I met your mother, she and you have been everything to me."

"We both love you, Dad." Scott swallowed hard and fell silent.

The double four poster bed, where Paul lay, felt smaller than its true size. The room was a large rectangle, arranged with heavy Victorian furniture. Light streamed in from two oversized windows facing West with heavy drapes pulled back and light white shear curtains moving slowly in the late Summer breeze. Many personal items and photographs crowded the available space on shelves, dressers, or hung on all four walls.

"The land."

"What?" Scott leaned towards his father's bed.

"The land, Scott, I said the land is what makes a man. It defines his character, even if he lives in a city, the land shapes man, not the other way around."

"What are you saying, Dad?"

205

"When someone from around here wants to know something about you, what do they ask?" The old man smiled and answered his own question. "They ask where you are from."

"I still don't see what you are trying to tell me." Scott sounded puzzled.

"You go off and camp in the forest, you know what it's like, don't you feel different when you're there?" Paul raised himself on one elbow. "Don't you feel different than when you're back here in town?"

"Yes, but that's why I like it, it reminds me of all the good times we had when I was a kid; it reminds me of when you, me, and grandpa went upstate and camped."

"You've got somewhere else, another place, in your blood, Scott. And that's why I want to talk to you alone before I go. One more piece of unfinished business before I go." Paul took a short breath. "My life's got more than one unfinished part, Lord knows, but this part you share with me."

"Well?" Scott leaned forward on the edge of his chair, facing his father's bed.

"I traveled all over this country with your grandpa, and I enjoyed every bit of the time I spent with him, but somewhere else in my spirit kept calling me; I've never shaken it."

"What are you talking about, Dad, where else have you been?"

"I was born in Georgia, not Vermont. I didn't know my real daddy until I was sixteen, and I was raised in the worst poverty a person can have."

"But you aren't poor now."

"Lack of cash isn't the worst poverty. I've gone without food for a week at a time. The whole time I grew up we never had more than two dollars at one time but the worst poverty is the poverty of the spirit, it makes you look at the world all wrong. Even though I've spent the last part of my life with you and your mother trying to make up for things I did not do, it didn't work, it can't be done."

206

"Who raised you, if you didn't meet granddad until you were sixteen?"

"I was raised by two fine mulattos, first on a plantation, then on free land, both in Georgia."

"Am I colored?" Scott's mouth fell open.

"Color ain't where the shame is, son," Paul paused, took another breath and continued. "The shame is in denying who you are."

"Who am I?" Scott pulled his chair closer to his father's bed.

"You're the deep South; so you are soft and gentle with a mean streak buried so deep that when it comes out it will be the death of you. Learn to recognize it when it starts to surface. Know it for what it is."

Scott felt washed in fear for a second, his eyes opened wider and his lips parted to gather more air in his lungs.

"What did you do, what will I do?" he asked.

"Nothing, and that's the sorrow." Paul pointed to the dresser against the opposite wall. "Go bring me the small brown leather picture book in the top left hand drawer.

Scott silently retrieved the book of ragged, brown pictures, then he lay them beside his father, who had turned his face to the opposite wall.

"Here they are, Dad," Scott said.

"Open the book yourself, I've got the images memorized. It took me a long time to collect the eight pictures you see in that book, but these are all I have left of my past; they were my past, and now you need to know them too." Paul turned to his son and continued. "That first one was a considerable pain to get, I had to buy it from Sarah's sister-in-law. That fine old bitty hated the memory of Sarah Bellows Appleby so much that she stole the picture from her brother in order to sell it to me for money, after she found out that that I was her dead sister-in-law's bastard child. It's a tintype of my real mother, Sarah Bellows, your blood grandmother. Granddad, God rest his soul, seduced her during the Civil war. Sarah owned thousands of acres, and hundreds of

207

negroes. I was raised by two of them; they're the folks in the next two pictures."

Scott moved his jaw several times before words emerged, "I don't understand, if you were born to this rich white woman, why were you raised by these people?" Scott pointed to the pages in the brown book.

Ignoring the question, Paul continued, "The pictures of John and Mary Burns hung on my wall for years before my real Daddy came to get me. I remember those pictures so well, I even remember when they paid that photographer to take them, they were so proud. Until I was ten years old, I thought I was colored and I was convinced the white man was my enemy."

"But you're white." Scott objected.

"I am. I am from the same people, the same land that tried to kill me, and that did kill those fine folks who raised me. That tintype of the man you are looking at right now, he loved me like I love you, he was my father. The night riders, people the same color as you and me, lynched him on a calm, dark night. I had to look at my daddy hanging, dead, in the night."

"Is that the mean streak you were talking about?" Scott glued his eyes to his father's face.

"I lived only one side of the social life in the South, and I lived on the land common to both, but I never became part of it."

"But who are these people, Dad?" Scott turned the page of the book.

"They're the Rose family, they were my salvation; it's taken me a lifetime to realize what they were teaching me. Some of them are still alive, I keep in touch with them. Their eldest son, Mark, was killed by the same men who killed my father."

"That is terrible," Scott stammered, looking bewildered.

"Two of Mark's brothers left the mill, Paul said. "They work in a college town as merchants."

"Is that the man you call Zeke?" Scott asked. "I've heard you telling Mother about him and his brother and their families."

"Yes, those are Mark's brothers. Their family is having a hard time with their mill and farms. I have been helping them for the past few years, and I think they will relocate on some land which will better suit their needs now. I own that land, but my lawyer is deeding it to them right now; our family will hold title to what's left of their old acreage."

"Wait," Scott sounded lost. "What are you talking about?"

"I have been buying up land in that area for years. If you can, keep it. If not, at least go live there first before you decide what to do." Paul closed his eyes and sighed. "I'm tired now." He opened his eyes again and looked at Scott. "You at least need to go back there; you need to know who you are, and that land is where you'll find out. I never did go back to do that, and I've paid my entire life. I guess that's why I've tried to own as much of it as I can, but the land winds up owning me in the end." Paul took a deep breath. He closed his eyes, his breathing staying shallow and steady.

. . . .

"What did he mean?" Scott asked his mother. "What was all that about his living with sharecroppers in Georgia?"

"Your father's a private man." Cecelia looked at her son. "He didn't tell me much about this until this last time he became ill."

"What did he tell you?"

"I suppose he told you as much as he told me," she paused. "I wish he had told me all this sooner, then his burden wouldn't have been as much these last few months."

"You had to know about all that land he was buying," Scott insisted. "Where is it? Why do we keep it?"

"Yes, I've known." She nodded slowly. "Your father had many land holdings, he was a lot like your grandfather; they both believed land was the one thing that couldn't be manufactured. Both your father and grandfather believed there was no greater long term investment than land."

209

"What about those coloreds he said raised him?" Scott sounded anxious.

"I wouldn't worry about that." His mother hugged him. "That was a long time ago and I think your father is trying to settle everything in his mind before he passes on."

"Don't say that, mother." Scott pulled away from his mother.

"You need to be patient with your father, he loves you very much."

"I want him to be here when I get married, I want him to know his grandchildren."

"He will be." Cecelia took her son back in her arms. "Maybe not like he is now, but he will be there for you."

Chapter 20

Everything passes, everything perishes, everything palls.
French Saying

"What the hell was that?" Billy lay John down in the road.

"What?" Al asked, looking behind them.

"Listen." Billy lowered his rifle. "Do y'all hear that?"

Tim cocked his head and listened to the forest. "Yeah. I hear people talkin', it sounds like they're everywhere, but real far off. It sounds like they're ridin' horses at a real slow pace too"

"Where?" Al asked in a whisper, grasping his rifle with both hands. "I can't tell where they are."

"Behind us," John said. "Someone pull me off this road and give me back my rifle."

Tim grabbed the two poles and pulled John into the forest beside the road, where he carefully placed John near a large red oak tree.

John confirmed that his rifle still contained ammunition; he made sure the safety was still on. He pulled the bandoleer of clips from his backpack and tossed it around his shoulder. Meanwhile, Al and Tim ran to the woods, heading closer to the noise. John unstrapped himself from the sling and rolled onto the ground to get behind the read oak. As Billy ran up the road, and then into the forest, the sound of voices grew louder, but no individual conversation was intelligible.

"Where are they?" Tim whispered to Al.

"Don't know, but keep lookin'." Al twisted his head around as far as it would go in all directions, looking intently into the forest.

Distant sounds of a small band of horses caught their attention. Next, they heard a brief musket retort and a soft whizzing sound over their heads.

"Run for the river," John called softly, not moving. "Run for the river." As his voice died off, a series of flashes and rifle blasts appeared to the left of the road, near Al and Tim's position. Immediately after the sound of many lead balls crashing through the forest, the voices came into focus; hoarse voices shouted commands to each other, none seemed to be in charge.

"Kill them niggers, get 'em off our land, kill them dirty bastards," One voice shouted, louder than the rest.

Billy leapt from his hiding place and ran back down the road.

"Shit, someone's shootin' at us, I can't see a damned one of them, but I sure hear their guns."

Al called back, "Billy! Over here."

Billy dove into the forest.

"I hate this." Billy ducked behind the fallen tree next to Al and Tim. "I can't see nobody, ain't nobody to shoot back at, I hate this."

"John!" Tim shouted as the sound of muskets came back, followed by the loud whisper of more bullets in flight.

The three men ducked, they placed their hands and arms over their heads. Bullets hit further up the road, scattering dirt and bark several yards away from them.

"John," Tim shouted again. "Are you all right?"

"So far," John's voice answered.

John sounded farther away than the last time they heard his voice.

"I'm gonna go get him," Tim said as another volley flew in.

Al pushed Tim's head to the ground as more incoming bullets hit trees around them with dull thuds.

"No you ain't, you'll get blown away for sure if you run around; he needs to stay low 'till the shootin's over," Al paused, waiting for the next incoming round of fire. "John and I've been

212

in the army, and you two haven't, so listen to me, he knows what to do to stay alive, and he'll do fine."

Partially muffled by the sound of rifle and some pistol fire, John's voice called, even more distant than before, "Make for the river now, move now."

More gunfire crashed through the forest; first three shots, then two.

"Them's muskets for sure," Billy said quickly. "They don't make too much noise, 'n you can hear the cap go off before the main charge, but what the hell's goin' on, why they want us dead?"

"We gotta get John," Tim said. He called out to John again.

"I said, get to the river, now," John shouted back. "I'll win this fight; this is my fight, go away." They still could not see him.

More musket shots echoed, then the loud retort from John's rifle answered them. He got off four more rapid shots before they heard several musket shots answered him.

"I don't care what you say," Tim said loudly. "I'm gettin' him right now."

Tim stood, held up his rifle and began to run for the road and John.

Al stood, looked for a second and shouted, "Let's do it." Billy followed him; they all reached the road simultaneously and stopped. John was gone. The forest fell silent once again.

"I said go to the river," John's voice repeated, from somewhere far into the forest to their right.

The outlines of trees along the road began to blur. The sound and projectiles were emphatically real as the sharp sulfuric odor of burnt black powder burned into their noses. Everything else was fading, blending into an even gray fog. They still could not see any men behind the rifle flashes and smoke.

"Where are you?" Tim demanded in a loud voice.

"Gone," John replied.

His rifle fired three more times; the metallic ring of the empty clip reverberated as it ejected, followed by the solid clank of John inserting a new one.   They heard the bolt slam close. Another round followed, rapid shots from John's rifle, then one or two musket shots.

"Which way?" Al shouted. "Where is he?"

Al raised his rifle to his shoulder, looking for a target.

"I can't see shit out here, where the hell's all that noise comin' from?" Billy wailed.

Another musket volley began as Al, Tim and Billy frantically scanned the forest for their friend.

Billy shouted, "Hit the dirt."   The volley slammed into them. Bullets hit Al twice in the chest, Billy once in the abdomen, and Tim in the left arm, stomach, and chest.

The concussion threw them off their feet; all three landed in the middle of the road, unconscious.

Chapter 21

In this country American means white. Everybody else has to hyphenate.
Toni Morrison, Guardian (London, 29 Jan. 1992)

After Paul's death, it saddened her to do so, but Cecelia Barrington sold most of her late husband's land holdings in Georgia, Alabama and Florida to support herself and her son. Scott Barrington was accepted into Yale medical school. Scott was haunted by his father's last words; he lost himself in college, but he never could forget. In the summer between his first and second year of medical school, he acted on his curiosity and regret by taking a menial summer job on a farm in Georgia. He had managed to find work on the land his father had told him about on the last day of his life. For the next three years, Scott kept this summer job, more for the comfort it gave him than anything else. The year he graduated, Scott worked only for one month on the farm, before he began his residency in a Boston hospital on August first, 1922.

"Why would someone in medical school want to pick cotton and do all this hard work for the Summer?" A large, burly man wiped sweat off his leathery tan forehead with a grubby hand.

"I figure it'll help me when I graduate and set up a practice somewhere," Scott replied.

"What made you pick this place?" The question came from a tall slender black man to Scott's left.

"A long time ago some of my family lived near here." Scott bent over and picked up the post hole digger. "My father used to own a lot of land near here."

215

"He don't now," The larger man, a white man, George, flatly stated. "If he did, you'd be workin' on your own land right now, I reckon."

"I guess I would, but my father's dead and Mother had to sell off most all of it to live on and send me to school." Scott slammed the post hole digger into the hard red clay. "Dad's name was Paul Barrington."

"I remember that." George scratched his bristly chin. "Wasn't that long ago."

"Yeah," Scott paused, then looked at George. "My mother died last year."

"Sorry to hear that." The black man, Charlie, shook his head as he leaned on a long handled shovel. "So, why you workin' out here so far away from your home up North?"

"My Dad's family was from right here on this land." Scott stopped digging. "He was raised right here on this plantation; my grandpa and my dad spent some time down here."

"Is that why the owners put up with you so much?" George took the digger from Scott.

"Sort of." Scott pondered his answer. "My father was the illegitimate son of Sarah Appleby."

Silence gathered over George as he let out a breath of air and stopped his digging in mid stride, while Charlie looked directly into Scott's face and smiled broadly.

George studied Scott for thirty seconds, then decided on a question, "Did your daddy's relatives live here long?" Before Scott had a chance to answer, George fired another question. "Are you white?"

"Does it matter?" Scott answered carefully.

"Damn right it does, boy," George said, annoyed. "It matters a whole hell of a lot around here; can't say what it matters up where y'all moved to, but around here you'd better get it straight."

"My father left here when he was about fifteen, or sixteen." Scott noticed that Charlie was still grinning. "He came back down here later when he was an adult and bought up a lot

216

of the old plantation, he used to visit here a lot when I was a little kid."

"That ain't what we're talkin' 'bout here, boy and you know it." George leaned slowy into Scott. Waiting.

"Both my parents and grandparents were white, and one of them owned this place, lock, stock, and barrel, and the other one owned most of it at one time." Scott moved away and took the digger from George, slamming it into the shallow hole. "My mother sold it to the present owners about ten years ago, and that's why they let me come down here each Summer and work in the fields and sleep in the big house. I wanted you to know in case I never see you again."

"You ain't comin' back here no more?" George asked, satisfied with Scott's explanation.

"I have an internship with a hospital which starts in a few weeks, so I can no longer take time off to work down here."

"A what?" George demanded.

"An internship," Scott answered. "That's where I learn to be a doctor, it's a full time job with no vacations."

"Still don't know why you do it." George shook his head. "Someone who's gonna be a rich doctor, why would you dig holes in the middle of the Summer down here?"

"I wanted to get the feel of this place before I had to settle down somewhere else and never got a chance to come back here," Scott replied.

Scott leaned the digger against his chest while he pulled on a pair of leather gloves.

"Ain't much to it, is there?" The heavy set white man chuckled.

"Yeah, there is to me, I think I'll actually miss it when I leave in two weeks."

Scott slammed the post hole digger a little deeper into the hard red clay.

"Too much bull shit from the boss man?" Charlie teased in a whisper to Scott.

Scott looked at George, whose grin was fast becoming a scowl. "No, too much work, but even at that I'll miss the land around here, it's been like coming home for these last couple of years. I'll miss it, it's good here."

"That's 'cause you get to live up in the big house with your kind," Charlie commented. He looked sideways at Scott and shot him a friendly grin, then he looked at George, who had moved in front of both of them.

"They may have taken a shine to me, but that's not why I come back each year." Scott slammed the digger another half inch into the ground. "I like you guys as much as the folks who own all this."

"Ain't that sweet," said George.

"Ain't as much you, though." Scott gave the large man with a half smile. "I like the lay of the land down here; I'll miss the big white house, and the big people who work it."

"Well?" He looked at Scott. "Why don't y'all come back down here 'n be a doctor, we could use one right here, ya know?"

Scott studied George's lined face, then he looked at the black man's tired face.

"I don't know, I guess this isn't my home after all; I need to go where I feel I belong when all is said and done," Scott said.

"I think we'd better lay some holes in this land right now, boy," Charlie interrupted. He had been watching George's face twitching.

"Damn right, boy, now start diggin'." The heavy set white man returned to his grin, dribbling a small amount of tobacco juice from the corner of his mouth. "Pretend your takin' out a 'pendix."

George ambled off towards a pile of fence posts in a wagon several hundred yards from Scott and Charlie.

"Boy," Charlie spoke to Scott in a hushed, serious voice. "I know who your people was, I mean the folks who raised your daddy."

"I guessed you might," Scott said softly to Charlie.

218

"Didn't recognize that name, Barrington, but I know damn well who Paul Burns was, now I know who you is."

Scott looked surprised and happy. "That's part of why I came back here."

"Horse shit." Charlie looked hard into Scott's eyes. "You came back here to see who you is, I know what's goin' on inside you, boy, and don't let that white man's pride get into you. Your daddy was raised right, he just didn't know it."

Scott gave him a sharp glance. "How the hell do you know so much about me and my father?"

"Man who raised him was my daddy's cousin," Charlie said quickly with pride. "I know what went on, lots of us still remember; I'm only fifty 'n I remember."

"Most folks here don't know what I'm talking about when I ask them anything about my father, or any of the people he knew," Scott paused to lean against the digger.

"You ask the wrong folks, 'n you ask the wrong questions. Might be better if you do get back up North, you sure don't belong here no more, times ain't gonna change enough for that, boy.

. . . .

"It ain't no skin off my nose," Charlie sounded hesitant as he motioned for Scott to sit in the chair next to the window that looked out onto a bare patch of hard red clay. "But, if the Saunders catch you socializin' with the coloreds too much, they's likely to run you out of town."

"I'm headed out of town anyway, so what's the harm?" Scott asked.

"Depends on what you ask."

"Right now, all I'm asking for is an introduction." Scott looked towards an older woman sitting on a two seat sofa across the living room from him. "Hello ma'm, I'm Scott Barrington."

"My name is Louise Burns," The woman spoke softly. "You can call me Auntie Lou."

219

"She's my aunt." Charlie looked hard at Scott. "She's seventy one this year and you take care in what you ask her."

"Don't be so hard on the boy," Louise chided Charlie. "He's family, and that's what he's come to find out about."

"What can you tell me?" Scott looked at the woman in front of him, not knowing what to expect.

"First of all." Louise leaned back in the sofa and paused to take in another breath. "I was born seven years after John Burns, the man who was your grandfather."

"You were related to him?" Scott asked.

"We had the same grandparents," she answered. "John was my first cousin."

"They was both born slaves on this plantation," Charlie interrupted. "This plantation that Sarah, your real grandma, owned, she owned your grandfather, and my Auntie Lou, both."

"Don't go bothering the boy," Louise scolded Charlie. "It wasn't his doings, besides I'm real impressed he's here asking these questions."

"I gotta ask why are you here askin' about all this?" Charlie demanded.

"I don't know," Scott paused. "But it felt important to my father. I started out following his last request."

"Why?" Louise asked.

"My father was about fifty three when he passed away and he told me all about John Burns and his wife Mary and that he was the illegitimate son of Sarah Appleby; he told me all this on his deathbed."

"That ain't nothin' most folks who've been here long enough don't know already," Charlie interrupted. "Things like that don't never show up in books, but folks talk about it. I remember my folks talkin' about it and I tell my kids; our history is passed on that way 'n nobody can take it away from us."

"I want to understand it more myself." Scott looked from Charlie to Louise, then back to Charlie.

"John Burns was lynched by the Klan in 1878," Louise sighed. "I remember that year, it was full of heartache for me.

My daddy died that year, my sister died in childbirth and I lost a child that December too."

"I'm sorry." Scott didn't know what to say.

"Thank you." Louise accepted his condolences. "Mary Burns died in 1880, I think she died of a broken heart. She left your father to the religious folks at the mill and went back to work the fields; most folks say she went there to die."

"The Burns folk wanted to bring your father back here to raise, but his real father showed up and took him away," Charlie said.

"That was Ralph Barrington?" Scott asked.

"Yes, child," Louise answered. "We never did meet your grandfather; I understand he was in the Union Army when they came through here."

"Yes, yes he was," Scott added. "That part of my past was easier to figure out."

"What's not so easy?" Louise asked.

"Why my father became so obsessed about his colored roots here." Scott didn't feel comfortable anymore. "My father didn't want to talk about it much, I think he was still upset about all that when he passed away; it felt like he was unburdening everything on his son and I was not prepared to take it all in."

"I can understand that," Louise said. "But why are you here?"

"I don't know," Scott said, confused. "My father was afraid of something, and I'm maybe far enough away from it to, well, I don't know."

"It's unfinished business," Louise interrupted. "You have to finish the family business."

"I guess so."

"That still doesn't answer my question," Louise said.

Scott looked at her, startled for a moment.

"Why are you here?" She asked again.

"I never knew this side of my father, but he was locked into something about this place and I need to find out what that

221

was. That much has become clear over the last few years. If only for my own peace of mind."

"I remember your father." Louise didn't let her eyes stray from Scott's face. "I took care of Paul for his parents when they had to go out for business, I played with your father when he was young. I was not married yet myself, still a young woman, so I looked after youngsters for other folks. Paul Burns thought he was part colored like John and Mary, I guess he was ten or twelve before he had a clue different."

"That explains some," Scott said.

"We all know the white folks' business," Louise's voice became somber. "We know who's sleeping with who, and we know who puts on the white robes and hangs our men."

"You know that's not me." Scott sounded uneasy.

"That's not what I'm saying," Louise calmly replied. "They know our business and we know theirs; we all belong to the same land, and we all share the same history, it's this dance we all do about who's on top and who isn't."

"What are you saying?" Scott asked.

"Your father played both sides of that dance, he lost track of the tune and he lost sight of his history," Louise said. "Your family needs to make peace with what your father didn't finish. It would have been so easy for him but you and your children and their children will all have the same predicament, until at least one of you gets to the bottom of it all."

"You look tired, Auntie Lou." Charlie stood up.

"So I am." She stood up and leaned over towards Scott; she kissed Scott slowly on his cheek and spoke softly into his ear, "I love you, you are family, son."

. . . .

Scott established a medical practice in Wooster, Massachusetts. He married late in life, at the age of forty two; his wife, Shelia, was eighteen years younger. They tried to have children for years, and were finally parents when Shelia was 36, and Scott was 54.

Scott retired from medicine when he was 65, and became ill when he was 67. He never resolved the feelings his father expressed on his deathbed, but like Ralph, lost himself in his work and in his small family. He looked to the Barrington family for comfort and ties, yet he always felt pulled South. He never traveled south of Pennsylvania since his early stint of working on the Georgia farm. His regret about the place was displaced with neglect and more pressing obligations. He was fond of his wife and son, working hard to support them. Like Scott, John was an only child.

....

"Mamma." John looked at his mother. "How long will you be gone?"

"I don't know," Sheila answered. "Your father is so ill and I have to fly to Boston to be with him."

"Will he die?"

"He is ill." Sheila sounded quite sad. She didn't like to think about it, but her husband, Scott Barrington, was an old man who had suffered a severe stroke. Being much older than his son, Scott had been distant, felt ill at ease as a father; he was a generation older that the other fathers in John's peer group. John loved his father but had a difficult time expressing it.

"Do you think he will get better?" he asked meekly, not knowing how to feel.

A loud knock at the front door interrupted them.

"Wait here." Shelia got up from the sofa and headed to the front door; it was four thirty in the afternoon and she couldn't think of who would call at this time of the day.

"Are you going to say something, or do I have to wait out here on the porch?" Standing in the opened door, a tall large man grinned at them.

"Scott?" Sheila sounded stunned. "I thought you were in the hospital?"

"I think the news of my demise is a bit premature," Scott said, still grinning. "Can I come in?"

"Come in, come in," Sheila stammered, unsure of reality but so happy to see her husband.

"Had to come by and see you and my favorite son."

"But." Sheila hugged Scott as hard as she could. "I'm driving to Boston tomorrow to see you."

"I thought I'd save you the trip," Scott whispered in her ear as they hugged.

"I don't understand." Shelia backed up to see her husband, touching him again to make sure she wasn't dreaming.

Scott held out his arms as John ran towards him. They sat down in some nearby chairs. "Mom said you were sick, what happened?"

"You're not sorry to see me are you?" Scott playfully asked.

"Scott," Sheila interrupted. "What's going on?"

"I've only got a minute," Scott sounded serious. "I have a ride picking me up in no more than a few minutes, and I have something I need to tell both of you before I go back to Boston."

"Will you be in Boston when I get there tomorrow?" Sheila demanded.

"Yes."

"Are you going to be back in the hospital?" She felt a dread creep over her as she watched Scott's face grow anxious.

"I will be there when you arrive tomorrow."

"I'm glad you came to visit us, father," John broke into the conversation, still holding his father's hand.

"You don't think I'd pass up a chance to see you, do you." Scott smiled at John.

"What's so important?" Sheila said, trying to regain her composure. "Why couldn't this wait until I got to Boston, are you sure it's all right for you to travel?"

"More than all right," Scott assured his wife. "Can you listen to what I have to say, then I must get going."

"Okay." Sheila slowly sat down on the sofa and pulled John down with her.

224

"You're the third generation." Scott quietly looked at John. "My father was named Paul Burns and you need to know the family story."

"Scott," Sheila sounded upset.

"You must tell him," Scott responded to his wife. "He's almost fourteen now, and he needs to know."

"Know what?" John asked.

"You need to know that you have the power to bring our family home, you can bring peace to this family, more than any other generation." Scott started to say more, then stopped. "You can reconcile, and you can heal."

"Scott?" Sheila sounded on the verge of tears.

"I need to go now," Scott paused, taking in a deep breath. "Let me check out front and see if my ride is here."

Scott stood, looked at his family for a second then walked quickly to the front door.

"What's Father talking about?" John grabbed his mother's sleeve.

"I'll tell you in a minute." Sheila got up and headed to the front door.

She looked up and down the street; some children played in the yard across the street, Mr. Belkins had gotten home from the grocery store he managed and was parking his car in his driveway next door, but Scott was nowhere in sight, nor was there a taxi, nor a car of any kind in the street.

Sheila's first cousin, Edna, lived in Boston, a short ride to the hospital her husband was supposed to be in. Sheila planned to stay with her cousin while she kept vigil with Scott. Sheila raced to the den, fumbled through the desk until she found her address book then flipped to the page which held her cousin's phone number. Getting through to Edna's number, she exchanged greetings with Albert, her cousin's husband.

"Edna's at the hospital with your husband, can I help you?"

"Oh, no thanks, I'll call the room at the hospital."

"Do you need the number?"

225

"No, thanks, I've got it." Sheila's heart rate jumped; she could feel her heartbeat in her throat. She dialed the hospital number.

"Hello, this is Scott Barrington's room."

"Edna?" Shelia's voice was quiet.

"Sheila, is that you?" Edna spoke louder.

"Yes," Sheila paused. "How's Scott?"

"Sheila," Edna paused for what seemed an hour. "I'm sorry."

"He passed away?" Sheila began to cry.

"The doctors left the room." Edna took in a deep breath. "How did you know?"

"I can't talk now," Sheila sniffed. "I'll see you tomorrow and tell you everything."

Chapter 22

Tim was the first to open his eyes onto the faint gray morning. Snow was falling silently, covering the brown grass in front of him; he felt the sting of a cold blast of air on his bare cheek, his entire body caught in a deep, painful chill.   When he lifted his head slightly from the ground to see what lay near him, a small quantity of powdery snow fell from his back. He felt a sharp surge of pain run across the top of his head as he strained to lift up. Tim slowly turned on his side; resting his head back down on the cold ground, he slowly moved his eyes to scan in front of him.

As far as he could move his eyes to his left, he could see a faint column of pale smoke rising to a low bank of clouds. Silently he began to take inventory of his injuries by carefully trying to move each section of his body, starting with his feet.

As he slowly moved his right arm to his side, he heard voices in the distance.

"Help," Tim spoke with so little force that he almost didn't even hear it himself.   Clearing his throat, he tried again.

"Hey Sam," the distant voice said. "I think one of 'em's here."

Tim could hear the sound of boots crunching in the snow coming towards him, the approaching boots compacted snow with each step.

"Oh God, what's gonna happen now," he whispered to himself as the men, seeing him now, ran towards him.

Tim closed his eyes for a brief time, then opening them when he felt the warm breath of a man bent over his face and holding a bare hand to his neck.

"You've got a strong pulse and you aren't too cold," the man said. "Do you think anything's broken?"

"I don't think so, my head hurts like hell, that's all." Tim looked up. The man leaning over him wore a dark green coat with a bright orange vest over it; he had a dark, weather worn face with a full beard, speckled with gray.

"What about my friends?" Tim said, suddenly remembering them. "They must be near here, are they all right?"

"I don't know, Sam's out looking for them now," the man assured him. "He'll find them and I'm sure they'll be all right too."

The man looked up and scanned the area then looked back down at Tim.

"Are you warm enough?"

"Yeah, I guess so. How long have I been out?"

"Some time," The man cautiously answered. "Looks like you've been out for some time. Oh, I think Sam's located them over there." The man stood up. "Wait right here while I go look at your friends, I'll be back in a second."

"Oh God, what happened?" Tim heard the two men talking in the distance, but couldn't understand what they were saying.

When a third voice joined the other two, Tim smiled as he recognized Al's voice.

The bearded man returned to Tim, looking down at him. "I'm the forest ranger for this district. Some other hunters reported to us about the explosion and the fire so we looked for you some last night, but with the storm, we called it off. You're lucky you had all these clothes on, you stayed warm enough; Sam found your friends, and they're all right, they're a little banged up and cold like you, but all right."

"They're all right?" Tim's voice showed relief. "Nothin' broken or nothin'?"

228

"I don't think so, but all of you'll have to be taken to the hospital for tests and x-rays," The man said. "How many of you are there? We only found three of you in this area."

Tim slowly shook his head and lifted himself up on his elbows while the forest ranger leaned over and placed his hands against Tim's back to help him rise to a sitting position.

"I was telling Sam that I knew something was going to happen yesterday, and I even knew the area it was going to happen in." The bearded man held on to Tim as he righted himself cautiously. "It was a real funny feeling, about a car wreck, like you guys had."

"Ouch." Tim blinked his eyes and tried to move his head in a slow shaking motion. "I'm sorry, I wasn't listening, I hurt too much."

"Be careful, there." The ranger gently placed his hand on Tim's shoulder. "Don't try to go any further, you might have some internal damage."

"That's all," Tim sighed.

"What?" The ranger asked.

"That's all of us," Tim said to the ranger. "Only three of us came up here, we was lookin' at the creek down there, through all this new cut land." Tim pointed to the clear cut slope leading down to the creek. "I lost control of the van 'n it slid down there 'n wrecked."

"Well, you're damned lucky you're all alive. Do you remember getting out of the van before it burned?"

"Not at all," Tim sounded puzzled. "I don't remember a thing after we started sliding."

"Well, you all sure are lucky, that's all I can say." The ranger stood back up and stretched. "With all the hunters in these woods, I knew something was going to happen today. I told my wife and Sam, he's my partner, yesterday that I was going to run this road this morning because I bet something was going to happen."

Tim looked up at the ranger. "You live around here?"

229

"Yeah, my wife and I live close by here; you go to the end of the Rose Community road, then take a left, we're the first house you get to, past the ruins. My family's lived around here forever, both our families go way back around here," The ranger paused for reflection. "Yeah, the Rose Community has been home to my family for three generations now, going on four."

"Oh yeah, that Rose place." Tim softly rubbed the back of his head with his right hand. "That's that little National Forest park, right?"

"That's the one," The ranger replied. "You look mighty familiar, have I seen you out here before?"

"I'm sorry." Tim extended his right hand to the ranger. "My name's Tim Masters, and thanks for being here so soon to help us."

"That's okay, it's my job. My name's John Burns, and I'm glad to meet you."

The Author

Bob Henneberger has been writing for the past decade, working mostly in Science Fiction and Mystery, He has also written short stories, plays, television scripts and articles for professional journals. He lives in Vermont, close to Lake Champlain with his wife and several cats; not that that's an indication of anything unusual.

www.ingramcontent.com/pod-product-compliance
Lightning Source LLC
Chambersburg PA
CBHW070821180626
46818CB00001B/349